Sister Wolf

The Southern Appalachian Mountains are full of secrets and unexplainable things. The story of Sister Wolf is one of them . . .

Mary Leslie Betts

Sister Wolf

Copyright ©2022 Mary Leslie Betts

ISBN 979-8-218-10659-1   Print
ISBN 979-8-218-12061-0   Ebook

Cover and interior illustrations by Rhonda Nadzeika

Book design by Nan Barnes, StoriesToTellBooks.com

Sister Wolf

CONTENTS

Dedication

I dedicate this book first to the Creator, as without Him, nothing would be possible. It is also dedicated to my family, my parents, Frank McLain and Mary Elliott McLain, for their influences in my life; to my ancestors, the McLains, Andersons, Elliotts, Ryans, Whelans, Lynches, and the others I do not know, for without them and the fateful joining of their lives, I would not be here; to my husband, Marty Betts, my son, Matt Villei, his wife, Kara, all who bless my life; and to my brothers, Mike McLain and Terry McLain, my sister, Lisa Ash, and their families; to my first husband, Chuck Lawlis, who taught me about life, not to fear death, who helped to make me a stronger woman, and who changed my life forever. It is also dedicated to my adopted brother and sister, Terry Red Hawk Harris and his wife, Nancy White Feather Harris, who helped to set us on the Red Path, and who have inspired me to greater things in this life; to our Sensei, Master Ed Johnson of Fort Worth Texas, who came into our lives when we needed him and who has made such an important impact on Marty, me, and our karate students. He has also set us on another path, like our Métis path, yet different. The end of the journey will be the same. Together with Terry Red Hawk, Sensei Johnson continues to inspire us spiritually. And, finally, this book is also dedicated to the Florida Frontiersmen, who created a place and time for us to cross paths with Terry Red Hawk and to be a part of the Alafia River Rendezvous, which has, in turn, been a special place for my spiritual learning for several years and an opportunity to be with our Métis brothers and sisters.

Life is a series of fateful events, which shape and mold the outcome, yet with only one change in one of those links, our lives would be different. Thanks to the Creator, for having the wisdom to allow these "chance" meetings and for the blessings He continues to give us daily. A'ho.

Mary Sister Wolf McLain Betts

Mary Leslie Betts

Chapter 1

SISTER WOLF

January 14, 1848

The young man sat by the bed of the old woman, watching her as she slept. Matthew was filled with emotions, for this woman, his great-grandmother, was about to die. She was more than his great-grandmother, though; she had raised him as her own after his own mother died during his birth. His father, her grandson, never remarried, so this woman was the only mother he had ever known.

Although she was ninety-five years old, she still had a hint of the flaming red hair she had been known for in her youth. Matthew sat by her bed, holding her hand, and thought of the tales she had told him as a young boy in this very house. He had started writing down these tales as soon as he had learned to read and write and now felt remorse for not asking more questions of her when he had the opportunity. Although what she had related to him sounded unbelievable, almost far-fetched, he knew that everything she had told him was true. He had seen things when they were together that defied explanation, yet they did happen.

He remembered the story of the wolf; she had called him her brother. She had saved the young wolf's life, and they soon became inseparable. When asked why she kept a wolf for a pet, she explained that he was not her pet, he was her brother. He was wild but chose to stay with her. Her relationship with the male wolf was the reason the Shawnee called his great-grandmother "Sister Wolf."

Matthew drifted off to sleep, only to be awakened by the howling of a wolf, a sound not heard in this part of the country in over fifty years, not since the Great Wolf Kill of 1796. It startled him from his deep sleep, and he wondered if he had been dreaming. He checked on his grandmother first. She was still breathing, but he knew it wouldn't be long before she crossed over. He stepped out onto the front porch and listened for any sounds. No creatures were stirring in the middle of winter in this part of western Virginia. The air was crisp and cold, and he could see his breath. He hurried back inside to stoke the fire and wait for Mrs. Ice's arrival in the morning. She was a local woman who knew a little about the white man's medicine. He knew his great-grandmother would prefer her Shawnee medicine, but all the Old Ones were gone—Red Hawk, White Feather, Walking Owl, White Bear. No one was left alive to help his beloved great-grandmother. For now all he could do was light her sage, say the prayer the old woman had taught him as a child, and make sure her medicine pouch was around her neck.

The old cabin was warming up after he added more logs to the fire, and he felt drowsy again. As he once more drifted off to sleep, he dreamed of the tales his great-grandmother, Mary Sister Wolf Ryan McLain, had woven into her daily lessons of life.

Chapter 2

MICHAEL RYAN

May 5, 1762

Michael Ryan wasn't a big man, but he was strong and compact. He was normally a quiet man, slow to anger, but not a man most would want to deal with once angered. Unlike a lot of the immigrants from the Emerald Isle, he didn't have the red hair the Irish were known for. With his dark hair, he was more of "Black Irish," but his eyes were emerald green. His daughter, Mary, had his green eyes but the fiery auburn hair of her mother, Mary.

Michael and his daughter, Mary, were waiting to leave the ship that had brought them from their homeland to this new frontier. They left Ireland on his wife's birthday, May 5, and arrived in this new country over ten weeks later, landing in the Port of Philadelphia. It had been a long voyage to Philadelphia and they were both tired. Michael's wife, Mary, had died in childbirth with their daughter, and he had not remarried. Michael had been forty years old when his daughter was born, and he had counted on family in County Tipperary for help with raising his daughter, but he had been forced to leave when a dispute over his land left one man dead and Michael and his daughter without a home.

He knew of James and Anthony Mohan, who were from the same area of Ireland he was from. They had made this trip several years before to try their luck on the frontier of western Virginia, and they had offered him a place to stay in their camp at the mouth of Mohan's

Run. Michael had wanted to wait until his daughter was older before even thinking about making the trip, but the recent problems in Ireland had forced him to leave before he and Mary were ready.

He didn't have much money and was in a new and strange place. He had heard of charlatans in this new world who would con a man out of his life's savings, so he was suspicious of everyone. He also knew he had to protect his daughter because, without him, she had no one else here who cared about her. Michael had a brother, John, whom he hadn't seen in several years, who he thought was living at Fort Loudin in Pennsylvania. Michael was anxious to find him. He had much to do before they could begin their travels from Philadelphia to the frontier of western Virginia.

The Mohans had been helpful. They gave him the name of a local woman who would give them a room for the night and help them find a guide to take them to their new home. As soon as they disembarked, Michael and Mary walked over two miles to Mrs. Elliott's house. It was well after dark and he hoped it wasn't too late.

As he stepped onto the porch to knock, the door opened and Mrs. Elliott burst through the door, "You must be Michael and Mary. I am sure you are hungry, please come on in."

She was a small, older woman—Ryan estimated she was in her fifties—but she was still pretty and had a smile that never left her face. Ryan was happy to be in her company. It was a welcome relief from the crowded ship and anxious passengers.

He could smell food and realized just how hungry he was. Mary and Mrs. Elliott hit it off right away. She showed them to their room, a small but clean room upstairs with two small beds, then told them to come downstairs to the kitchen and she would fix them a plate.

Father and daughter put their meager belongings in their room and started to descend the stairs together. As they did, a young man came from the room next to theirs and joined them. "Hello, you must be Mr. Ryan," the young man said. "I'm Frank Anderson. Mrs. Elliott explained your situation, and I offered to help get you to your destination in Virginia."

Michael was surprised and worried at the same time. He needed help, there was no doubting that fact, but he had no idea what it would cost for this stranger to get them to the Mohan's camp. "Mr. Anderson," Michael explained, "I don't have much money after paying for our passage from Ireland. I would appreciate any advice you can give me, but I'm not sure I could pay you to take us there."

The younger gentleman smiled before he answered. "Don't worry about my fee. I need to go in that direction myself and would be happy for your company. We can discuss it over dinner. Please call me Frank."

Michael Ryan smiled, relieved, and answered, "Call me Michael."

The three of them entered the dining room together just as Mrs. Elliott was putting the food on the large table. Michael offered to say grace before the meal, and Mrs. Elliott thanked him. Father and daughter savored their meal; it was the best they had eaten in months.

Mrs. Elliott was the first to speak. "I see you two gentlemen have met. Mr. Ryan, I hope you take Mr. Anderson up on his offer. He stays here when in town, and I happened to mention to him that you had written in your letter that you and Mary needed to travel to western Virginia. Mr. Anderson will take good care of you."

Michael swallowed before answering, "Yes, thank you, Mrs. Elliott. We've talked briefly. I can't afford to pay much but appreciate what he can do for us."

"As I explained, I won't take any money from you," Frank interjected. "I'll get you there as quickly as I can, but you will have to pay for your passage if we travel down the rivers. Most of those people know me, however, and I can get you a discounted rate."

"Thank you, Frank," Michael said.

The two men talked while Mary helped Mrs. Elliott clear the table and clean up the kitchen. Frank explained to Michael the route they would take south, then west toward their destination. When Mrs. Elliott and Mary entered the room, Frank explained they would be leaving early in the morning, and they needed to get their rest. Mrs. Elliot would fix their breakfast and make food for them to take on their journey.

Frank and Michael shook hands, and Mrs. Elliott hugged Mary and told her to have sweet dreams, but Mary said she was too excited to sleep. She couldn't help but think of the adventures that awaited her in this new land.

When Michael thanked Mrs. Elliott and tried to pay her, she would not take any money from him. "No, she said. "You save it for your trip."

Michael felt the tears welling up in his eyes. "God bless you," he said. He hoped all the people he met in this new land would be as kind as Mrs. Elliott and Frank Anderson.

It wouldn't be long before he would find that would not be the case.

Chapter 3

HERMIT EEDS

August 1762

Robert Eeds and his wife lived in a cave on a stream called Hermits Run, close to Mohan's Camp. Locals believed they had arrived in this part of western Virginia as early as 1742 or 1743. Robert's family had previously lived in a cave near the Cacapon River, but Shawnees found their cave, took the entire family captive, and took them across the mountains to an Indian town on the Ohio River. There, they murdered his eight children—four boys and four girls—and tortured him and his wife for a year. The Shawnees hated him because he had killed at least fifteen of their people while he lived in the Cacapon country. He would set traps for the Indians; he called the traps "leg-breakers." He would follow the trail left where those caught in one of the traps had crawled away and then kill them with an axe.

Eeds was seventy-three years old, tall, and bony, with long gray hair and a beard that hung to his waist. He had big black eyes that burned holes right through you. He slept on a bed of bearskins and ate mostly bear meat, mussels, greens, and bread made from beech-nuts and other nuts pounded into meal.

After Eeds and his wife escaped from the Indians west of the Ohio River, they journeyed back to western Virginia. He found the cave at the mouth of Hermit's Run, and they lived there quietly for twenty years. During that time, Eeds didn't kill as often as he would have liked, but once his wife died, Old Man Eeds took out his revenge on any Indian who came through his territory. He was hell-bent on ridding western Virginia of every Shawnee. Since his wife was gone, he didn't have to worry about what would happen to her if he died in battle with one of the murderous savages who had taken the lives of his beloved children.

Every time he fought and eventually killed each Shawnee, he would say, "This is for my little Catherine," or "This is for my little Robert," as he landed the fatal axe blow. Each time it would be a different name as he did his dirty deed. Eventually, he lost count of the number he had killed; he just knew he had said the names of each one of his children three times over since escaping from the Shawnee. Just before killing the last one, a young man of sixteen, Eads said his wife's name. "This is for my Elizabeth!" It didn't matter to Old Man Eeds that this boy—or any of the other ones he killed—weren't the ones who murdered his children. Most of them weren't even alive then. He just wanted someone to pay, and someone did.

Eeds had spied on the Mohans for years. But it wasn't until Eeds' wife died and he became lonely that the Mohans even knew of his existence. He began to wander down to their camp to visit. As much as he hated to be alone, he also hated to be in the Mohans' camp when one of the murderous Shawnees were there to trade.

He was great at covering his tracks, almost becoming invisible. He had thirty years of practice in these hills. He hadn't strayed far from his cave during those thirty years, fearing discovery by the Indians, but he knew every inch of the land within a twenty-five-mile radius. Nothing happened that he didn't see or know about.

When people started coming to the area, he would watch them as they traveled the rough paths along the creek below his hideout. Along with the Mohans, he knew of the Falls, Ices, Nichols, Taylors, Pricketts, Duvalls, Leggits, and other early settlers to the mountainous land.

Today, just as Eeds came down the path from his cave to where he could see the valley below, he saw movement on the trail at the bottom of the hill. He stopped and watched with interest as a man and young girl made their way northwest towards the Mohans' camp. It was a bright August day in 1762. He was on his way to that same camp when he noticed the strangers' movement. The man was shorter than him, but stocky; the girl was about nine or ten, with bright auburn hair that shone in the morning sunlight. They walked at a quick pace, as if they knew they were close to their destination. Eeds watched intently, squinting his dark eyes as the two made their way on the trail. The girl reminded him of his beloved little girl, Catherine. Tears blurred his vision as he thought of her and how she had died.

Suddenly, the man on the trail below looked back at the girl then stopped as if sensing they were being watched. Eeds knew he hadn't made any noise or movement to give away his location, yet the man stared in his direction. Then he realized it was the girl who had noticed him first, and she must have said something to the man, who was probably her father. There was something different about that girl. Eeds couldn't quite put his finger on it, but she was special. He would find out just how special she was in the next few weeks.

As much as Eeds wanted to go to Mohan's Camp, he decided to wait until the next day. The strangers needed some time to settle in. He couldn't wait to meet the little red-headed girl. He didn't have many friends, but somehow, he knew she would be his friend. He didn't realize at that moment just how important they would become to each other.

Eeds waited until the strangers were out of sight before he turned and walked toward his cave. He stretched out on his bear-skins, something he didn't often do during the day, closed his eyes, and fell asleep. In his dreams, he saw the faces of his wife and little Catherine, who were both smiling at him.

He didn't wake up until daylight poured into his cave. Today would be the day he would meet the little red-haired girl.

Chapter 4

MOHAN'S CAMP

August 1762

Michael never saw Old Man Eeds on the hill looking at him as he hurried to reach the Mohans' camp before dark. He was tired and hungry, and although she didn't complain, Mary had to be too. The trip from Philadelphia had been exhausting, and now that they were so close to their destination, he just wanted to eat and go to sleep.

Michael had received directions from the Mohans and hoped the wide place on the path up ahead was where he was to turn right. He didn't want to make a wrong turn now. As father and daughter reached the turn off, a man appeared, waving, and hollering. "Michael?"

What a relief! It was Anthony Mohan. "It won't be long now, Mary, we are almost there!" Michael assured his daughter.

The two men shook hands, and Mohan bent down to greet Mary. At first she hesitated, after hearing all the lectures from her father about being wary of strangers, but she looked at her father and he smiled, giving her a nod to go ahead. She reached out and hugged the man, who picked her up, saying, "You must be tired, young lady. How about a ride to the camp?"

This started Mary to giggling as her new friend put her on his back and said it was her first horse ride.

Within ten minutes, the three rounded a bend and Michael saw for the first time what would become his new home. There were four cabins on the right side of the trail, and someone had a fire going. Michael could smell the roasting meat and could hardly contain himself.

"You must be hungry," Mohan said. "We have an extra cabin you can use for now, until you build your own. For now, let's get you both something to eat."

Michael couldn't help but notice how much this land, called Virginia, reminded him of his beloved Ireland. There were beautiful green hills, meadows that defied description, an almost sacred but eerie feeling in the ground below his feet. The only thing missing was the stone fences that surrounded the farmlands where he was born. This made him think of his wife, Mary, and for a second he thought he was home. He was brought back to reality by the clanging of a bell—the call to supper made by the old cook in the Mohans' camp.

Mohan set Mary on the ground, and the three walked toward the cook. It was still warm enough to sit around the fire while Michael, Mary, the Mohans, and the old cook feasted on the stew. Tonight, there weren't as many to cook for, as most of the others were out hunting. Michael didn't know if he was more tired than he was hungry, but the stew was delicious! At first, no one said anything; they were too busy enjoying their meals.

Anthony Mohan was the first to speak. "Michael," he asked, "how was your trip?"

Michael was slow to answer, partly because he didn't want to stop eating and partly because he was so tired. "I am so glad to finally be here!" he finally managed between bites. It has been a long journey from Ireland. Ten weeks on board the ship that sailed into Philadelphia and then the days spent getting here to Virginia. We travelled with Frank Anderson, who was able to get a horse and wagon and offered to escort us. We first stopped in Fort Loudin to inquire about my brother, John, but we found he had moved farther west. Then we headed west across very rugged country toward Fort Pitt, where we said our goodbyes to Frank and managed to get a ride on a small boat down the Monongahela River to Buffalo Creek. We followed the creek here." Altogether, including the time on the ship, traveling across Pennsylvania, the boat ride, and then more walking, Mike and his daughter, Mary, had been traveling over three months.

Anthony was amazed that this inexperienced man and young girl had managed such a trip. *Michael is going to fit in nicely here,* Anthony thought. He offered, "First things first. After dinner we'll make you comfortable for the night. Then we need to get you a flintlock and tools you'll need in order to survive here. We'll start cutting trees for your cabin, teach you about hunting and fishing, give you information on the Indians in the area, and introduce you to the locals."

Michael thanked him. He was anxious to be settled, build his own cabin, and become proficient in the skills necessary to live on this new frontier.

The group didn't linger at the fire for very long after their meal. Anthony knew Michael and Mary were tired, so he showed them to their temporary cabin and told Michael that breakfast would be ready at dawn. Then he bid them goodnight and closed the cabin door.

No words were spoken between father and daughter when Michael picked up Mary and hugged her to his chest. Mary did not see the tears in her father's eyes but knew what he was thinking. "Papa, I know. I also wish Mam were here with us!"

Michael held on a little longer then looked into the knowing eyes of his daughter. How did she know what he was thinking? He kissed her on the cheek, put her down, and said, "Goodnight, my angel."

"Goodnight, Papa."

Chapter 5

BUFFALO CREEK

1762 –1763

Michael and Mary were up early the next morning. Despite being tired from their long journey, both were anxious to explore their new homeland and learn the ways of the frontier. The old cook was up well before dawn as well, and Michael could smell breakfast cooking. He and Mary changed from their nightclothes, made their beds, and tidied up the cabin before joining the rest of the camp by the fire.

The Mohan brothers, Anthony, James, and John were already sitting by the fire when Michael and Mary arrived. "Did you sleep well, my friend?" asked Anthony.

"Yes," said Michael. "Thank you."

The men weren't used to having too many females around, especially as young as Mary, but they soon took a liking to her and enjoyed teasing her. They seemed to like to see who could make her blush red first.

James Mohan was the first to talk to Mary that morning. "Well, lass, did you sleep well too?"

"Yes," she answered meekly.

"You better git your tummy full of vittles first, then we will see about gittin' your Pa a gun and some other tools."

"Thank you."

Mary and her father began eating the breakfast the old cook had prepared, not sure what was expected of them by the rest of the camp. Michael was happy to hear that he might be getting a gun but was worried about what it would cost. He did not have much money left after their trip from Ireland.

"James," Michael said. "I don't have a way to pay for a gun just yet."

James told him not to worry, they would find something for him to do to help work off the debt.

The Mohan brothers took turns explaining to Michael how they had recently claimed this land and began trading with the friendly local Indians. They made this their permanent home and built four small cabins here at the mouth of Mohan's Run where it joined Buffalo Creek. James began to tell them about a local man who lived in a cave nearby, Robert Eeds. Eeds was known as "Old Eeds" or "Hermit Eeds" by the locals. "Old Eeds is a queer one," James Mohan said.

Amazingly, as if on cue, Eeds stepped out of the woods and approached the group around the fire.

Michael couldn't help but stare and at first didn't notice that Mary had stood up and was walking toward the old man. "Mary! Stop!" Michael yelled.

Eeds had seen similar reactions from people when they first saw him, but he was more fascinated with the young girl than her father, and it was obvious that she was fascinated with him.

James quickly calmed the situation down. "Good morning, Mr. Eeds. Would you like something to eat?" He pointed to Michael and then to Mary and continued. "Let me introduce you to our new neighbors, Michael Ryan from Ireland and his daughter, Mary.

Old Man Eeds reluctantly put his hand out to shake Michael's hand, but his eyes were on Mary. He fought back the tears as he thought again about how much she resembled his Catherine.

Eeds forced a smile when Mary offered him a seat beside her in spite of her father's obvious disapproval. The old man got his plate of food from the cook and sat beside the little girl. They quickly became acquainted and began talking like they were old friends. Michael couldn't keep his mind on the conversation with the Mohans; he couldn't take his eyes off his beloved daughter.

The Mohans watched Eeds as he talked with Mary and were surprised. It was the first time they had seen a smile on the old man's lined face. Little did they all know what a good friend this man would become, especially to Mary. He would teach her things and give her the skills she would need in later years.

Chapter 6

PAPA

May 1763

Michael Ryan felt uneasy. He was traveling with the Mohan brothers, Anthony, and John, and he knew that Mary was in the care of Anthony's wife, but he hated to leave her. She was all he had left from his life in Ireland and his wife, Mary. His daughter had tried to put on a brave face when he left earlier that morning, but he knew she was upset that she couldn't go along, and there was a look of fear in her eyes.

As the three men made their way along the well-worn trail, John Mohan kept looking back as if he saw or heard something. Just as Michael was about to ask him about it, Mohan raised his flintlock and took aim.

Michael looked in the direction of where the round ball would go and let out a half scream. "God, no, it's Mary!"

The three men watched as the young girl, slowly at first, crept out of the trees along the creek. Once Mohan had lowered his weapon, Mary ran to her father.

At first they just hugged. Michael had so many feelings washing over him at the same time—relief that Mohan had not fired, anger that his daughter would even think of traveling this far alone, and love for this young girl who saw only the good in people and animals, sometimes to a fault. He tried not to be angry, but he had to impress upon his daughter that she could not do this again. "Jesus, Mary, Mr. Mohan could have killed you!"

The young girl had never seen her father angry, let alone at her. "I'm sorry, Papa, I just wanted to be with you."

"Mary, you traveled alone for four miles!" Michael had no idea how she had kept up with the adult men. She must have left camp right after they did.

Michael knew he had no choice; he would have to abandon the Mohans and return to his cabin with Mary. He scolded her again and mentioned how upset Mrs. Mohan must be, not knowing where she had taken off to. He thanked John Mohan for his patience with his weapon and for not shooting his beloved daughter. He apologized for having to leave them, but they understood. He shook hands with the brothers and he and Mary started back to the camp, but Michael knew the Mohans would be talking about this for the rest of their trip. Some people might think Michael was too lenient with his daughter; others might be afraid of her after seeing the events that had happened since their arrival in Mohan's Run.

Both father and daughter were quiet for the first thirty minutes of their trip. Both were too deep in thought to notice the movement in the shadows of the trees. Mary was the first to notice, not because she saw or heard anything, but because she felt the presence of the dark strangers before they appeared.

"Papa!" The urgency in his daughter's voice broke her father's concentration on Mary's early morning behavior, and it was then that he noticed the barrel of a gun pointed at them. He quickly pushed his daughter behind a large tree that, thankfully, was close to the path. His loaded gun was by his side and ready to fire just as the blood-curdling yell came from the warriors as they broke through their woodland cover and ran toward them.

There were three warriors, and Michael would only have one chance for a shot. He chose the warrior in front. If he was lucky, the lead ball would go through the first one and hit the second one running closely behind the leader. Michael took aim, held his breath, and prayed the ball would find its mark. A split second after he squeezed the trigger, the gun fired, smoke filled the air, and he heard the thud of the bullet as it hit the first warrior dead center in his chest. It went clean through him, hitting the second warrior in his arm. Only one continued advancing toward them. Michael didn't have time to reload. He pulled his knife from its sheath and, with a prayer on his lips, stepped out to face the other man.

Although a small man, Michael Ryan was strong and experienced in the gentlemanly ways of boxing in his home country. But here, in this wild country, there were no rules when it came to a fight. His greatest strength came from his love for his daughter. He must protect her at all costs, and he must survive to continue to protect her.

Michael could see the first warrior was dead, the second one still on the ground, losing blood quickly. His opponent, though, was coming at him with a large knife. Michael would have to deflect any attack and counter with his own knife. To his horror, just as he raised his knife to thrust it into the chest of the man in front of him, Mary ran between them. This caused the warrior to lose his concentration for a split second, enough time for Michael to thrust his knife into the right side of the warrior's chest. As he did, blood came pouring out, hitting him and Mary. He quickly grabbed his daughter and flung her behind him to safety. He didn't turn his gaze from the Shawnee but yelled to his daughter, "Stay!"

Mary was crying now, but she sensed the urgency of their situation and remained where she was. As she watched, the two men continued to fight, both receiving wounds from the other's knife. After what seemed like an eternity, both men were exhausted. Both had lost blood, and both loss consciousness at the same time.

When Michael came to he couldn't believe his eyes. Mary had managed to bandage not only his wounds but the wounds of both Shawnee warriors. He tried to get up but became dizzy and sat back down just as the knife-wielding Shawnee regained consciousness. He too started to get up but stopped. It was apparent that he was not feeling any better than Michael. His face changed from anger to amazement as he realized the young girl had tenderly bandaged all three of the men; he had never seen anything like this.

The third Shawnee was now also awake and the two spoke in short sentences. The one he fought knew enough English to make them understand they were now captives, and they would all be traveling west and taking the dead warrior with them. Since they outnumbered him, Michael had to go along with what they were demanding. Somehow, Mary had managed to hide the knives and guns, and no matter how hard they tried, neither her father nor the warriors could get her to tell them where they were.

The two warriors managed to make a travois to carry their companion, even without their tools. It was Michael's job to drag the corpse, a challenging task, especially with his own wounds. They started on their journey, heading the same direction they had just come from— toward the Ohio River. It was not easy going, as the hills were steep and Michael was weak. After walking for about four hours, the warriors indicated they were stopping to rest. One warrior stayed with Michael and Mary as the other one took their water bags with him up the hill. When he returned, they had fresh, cool water to drink. They made camp, ate cold food, and slept at the base of the hill for the night.

When they left in the morning, Michael was able to see the source of water. One warrior explained that it was a spring and the ancient ones had managed to bore a hole through the rock to get to the water. Mary was excited about the story and didn't stop asking questions, but the story only briefly distracted her father from the serious thoughts running through his mind. Michael had heard stories of what happened to captives upon their arrival in the Indian towns. All he could do was pray.

Chapter 7

SIMON GIRTY

May 1763

The trip westward with the Shawnee warriors was the worst three days of Michael Ryan's life. He was in so much pain that he was almost delirious. More importantly, he was concerned about what would happen to his daughter when they reached their destination.

Mary stayed right beside him all the way, with one warrior behind the travois carrying the body of the dead man and the other one leading the small party. When they stopped to rest and eat, the warrior in the lead motioned for the young girl to come to him. At first she hesitated, then she slowly took a couple of steps toward the man who had tried to kill her father.

Michael held his breath, afraid to speak. He didn't want to frighten Mary or make the warrior angry, but he was ready to jump if he thought his daughter was in danger.

The warrior cut a piece of dried meat and handed it to Mary, then motioned toward her father.

Mary obeyed, giving the meat to her papa. She returned to the warrior, who cut a piece for her, handed it to her, and smiled. "Thank you," she said.

He nodded his head as if to say, "You are welcome." Something about this young girl had softened the warrior, but Michael was still on edge.

When the party arrived at the village, the captives quickly became the center of attention. The noise became more than either of them could bear. Men, women, and children poked and prodded them. It was all Michael could do to not hit every one of these savages who touched his daughter. Before things got out of hand, a man came into the crowd—Michael thought he must be a chief— and began talking to the two warriors who had brought in the captives. Even though Michael did not understand their language, he knew what they were saying by the expressions on the faces of the three men and the crowd around them.

Now it was known that Michael had killed one of their warriors and wounded the other two. It was obvious the warrior who had fed them was now telling his chief about Mary and how she had cared for them. He was smiling as he pointed to Mary then showed his chief his bandages. In spite of this, Michael got a very disturbing feeling in his chest, but he blocked out any thoughts of what might happen to him. His only thought, his only purpose in life at this moment, was to protect his daughter.

The crowd grew angry around them. Two women grabbed Mary and quickly took her to one of their wigwams away from the center of the village. Four men ran to Michael and grabbed him. Two war- riors stripped Michael of his shirt, then painted his body black and started pulling him toward a stake in the middle of the village, where they tied him. Three of the younger boys grabbed pieces of firewood and began to spread them around the stake where Michael was tied.

Hoping she could hear him, Michael cried, "Mary, I love you! It will be all right!"

Just then one of the warriors hit Michael on the head with a long piece of firewood, knocking him unconscious.

The chief, Red Hawk, yelled for the warrior to stop. "I know you want to avenge your brother's death, but that is not the way to do it!"

A man stepped out of the shadows, a white man, dressed as the Indians were, with a long-sleeved shirt, leggings, breechcloth, and moccasins. He must have been a powerful man among the savages because they seemed to listen to him. He spoke in their language, pointing to Michael and the trail leading into the village.

Michael was beginning to regain consciousness. If he could have understood what the white man was saying, he would have appreciated that the man was saving his life. The man was asking for the Shawnee to let Michael eat, rest overnight, and tomorrow, when he was stronger, then he could run the gauntlet.

After the chief spoke to the white man, a warrior and the white man untied Michael. The white man told him that his name was Simon Girty. Michael couldn't believe the man who had spoken in his defense was none other than Simon Girty, the renegade! Although Michael had only been in western Virginia for a short time, even he had heard of the infamous man.

Girty explained what would happen tomorrow: Michael would run the gauntlet. He explained that Michael would be forced to run between two rows of Indians who would strike him with sticks and other weapons. If he survived, the Shawnee would adopt him, and he would be allowed to live.

Michael thought it was just prolonging the inevitable, but the fighting spirit in him reasoned that this request might just give him a chance to escape. One of the warriors took Michael to the wigwam where two women were holding Mary.

Chapter 8

THE GAUNTLET

May 1763

Michael and Mary were fed by the two women, and bedding was laid out for them in the wigwam. There was always a warrior outside the opening, so there was no chance of escape. Michael knew he should try to sleep in order to gain what strength he could muster for what he would face the next day, but he could hear the warriors outside around the large fire, the one he would have been burned in if not for Simon Girty. The warriors were drumming and dancing around the fire in anticipation of tomorrow's event.

Michael spent a restless night, the pain in his body so severe that he could not find a comfortable position. For a brief time, he slept and dreamed of his new home, western Virginia, and how happy he had been at the Mohans' camp with Mary. But then his dreams took him back to Ireland and his beloved wife, Mary. Just as he reached out to embrace his wife, the face of the warrior he killed hung in the air above him, his face contorted in anger. The beauty of his late wife and his homeland disappeared. As he gazed at the image of the dead man's face, a dark, foreboding dread welled up inside Michael. He had to run the gauntlet tomorrow and survive. His daughter's life depended on it.

Michael was awake long before the women entered the wigwam to give them breakfast. He looked at the face of his daughter and silently gave thanks to God for her. She looked so much like her mother that tears formed in his eyes, but he quickly wiped them away. He had no room for weakness today. He must gather all his strength—physically, mentally, and spiritually—in order to defeat his foes.

After he woke Mary, they ate in silence. Mary knew her father's life was in danger. She got up from the floor, wrapped her arms around his neck, and gave him a quick kiss on his cheek. "Papa, you have the strength of ten men! God will be with you today! The angels will lift you up!"

Michael didn't have much time to think about what his daughter had said. Two warriors came into the wigwam, grabbed Michael by his arms, and took him outside where the entire village was waiting. They stripped off his shirt and painted his upper body black again. He could hear Mary yelling to him from inside the wigwam; she was not allowed to watch. One of the younger warriors was sitting in front of the door to keep her inside. "I love you, Papa!"

Michael quickly answered back, "I love you, Mary!" As he sized up the scene in front of him, he prayed silently, then remembered what she had said: *The Angels will lift you up.*

All the while, the villagers began to line up in two lines. Sometimes, the lines would be made up of women and young boys, all brandishing clubs, sticks, and poles. But today, both lines consisted only of warriors, all with tomahawks, knives, and clubs. At the far end of the two lines was a longhouse. If the captive could reach the longhouse, his life would be spared. If he fell, he had to start over at the beginning.

Simon Girty asked Chief Red Hawk if he could have a moment with the captive. Girty looked Michael in the eye and said, "Stay low, fight back, and reach the longhouse!"

Michael looked at the longhouse. It was a hundred yards from the starting line, but it looked more like a mile to him. There were warriors on both sides of the course eager to land a killing blow to his skull. At the end of the line, on the right side, was the warrior who had led the group of men who had tied him to the stake the night before. Michael knew that warrior would be his last obstacle to reaching the longhouse. Just then the signal to start was given by Red Wing.

Michael took off as fast as his wounded body would let him. He blocked blows to his head but was unable to keep the warriors from striking his body, arms, and legs. One warrior on the left struck at Michael's head with his tomahawk. Michael blocked the warrior's right arm with his left arm, grabbed the tomahawk, swung around, and hit the warrior in the ribs. Without breaking stride, he kept moving toward the longhouse, the tomahawk in his right hand. He managed to get through the lines without any serious blows until he reached the last warrior.

Hate flared in the warrior's eyes, more than the others, and he came at Michael with his war club in one hand and his tomahawk in the other. Michael knew he didn't have much strength left; he had exerted himself already, more than he would have ever believed possible. It wasn't just his life at stake; his daughter's life was also at stake. He took one step forward, jumped in the air, and struck at the warrior with all he had left. Mary's words came to him, as if she herself were there. *The Angels will lift you up!* Michael could not explain what happened then, nor could he for the rest of his life, but as he took that last step, it was if he stepped onto a solid object and his body was propelled into the air. He struck at the warrior, who had missed him with both his weapons, and Michael stuck his tomahawk into the man's left shoulder. The warrior yelled in anger as much as he did in pain and fell to the ground, and with no one else blocking his way, Michael reached the opening of the longhouse.

Chapter 9

RED HAWK
AND WHITE FEATHER

May 1763

Just as Michael reached the longhouse, Mary managed to get by the young warrior who was standing outside the wigwam to watch over her. She ran straight to her father, trying not to cry. She was relieved to see that he was alive. The villagers were still standing in their places, not sure what they had just seen. Simon Girty was the first one to reach Mary, then two women came to tend to Michael and his wounds. The five of them walked slowly to the wigwam, warriors who had hoped to kill this white man now moving out of his way with respect. Only one still wanted to kill him, Snapping Turtle, the last warrior in the gauntlet, the one Michael had wounded. Michael would soon find out he was the brother of Running Badger, the warrior Michael had killed when he and Mary were captured, and the father of Digging Turtle and Red Turtle.

As the father, daughter, and Simon walked toward the wigwam, Simon touched Michael gently on his shoulder. He knew from experience the pain Michael was in. Girty said, "Michael, I have been where you are now. Life with the Shawnee is not so bad."

Michael heard what the white man dressed as an Indian was saying, but he didn't believe it. He had heard of this Simon Girty from the Mohans; he was a renegade, turned against his own people. He would become known as "The White Savage," "The White Renegade," and "Dirty Girty." Later in life, Michael would recall this conversation. How could this man, so despised by so many, be capable of the kind acts he had seen these past two days? Michael owed him his life.

As the group settled in the wigwam, Simon told Michael of how the Indians had accepted him. Simon's father, Simon Sr., had been a Scotch-Irish packhorse driver and Indian trader. His trade had taken him away from home for prolonged periods of time, leaving his wife, Mary Girty, and their four boys to look after themselves. He had been a hard-working, hard-drinking, hard-fighting man and had died in a duel with a man named Samuel Sanders. It was difficult for his widow and the four boys after his death, so she eventually married an older man, John Turner, who was her husband's half-brother.

Turner supported the family but was very mean. He often became drunk or was angry about something and beat the boys or Mary. The boys hated their stepfather. In 1756 the Senecas took Simon and his stepfather captive. The Shawnee and Delaware took his mother and brothers. The Senecas tortured Turner to death in front of Simon. They adopted Simon, and he lived with them for eight years, during which time he became well-liked by Indians of different tribes and lived among them at various times. Luckily for Michael, Girty was with the Shawnee when he and Mary were brought to this village. Their lives were saved because of him.

Chief Red Hawk and his wife, White Feather, made their way to the wigwam where a woman named Willow was treating Michael's wounds. When they entered, Simon Girty stood up to show respect to the chief. Although Red Hawk spoke a little English, Simon translated. Michael also stood up, and Red Hawk began his talk. "You have shown your fighting spirit here today. You are a warrior. We mean you no further harm. I will take you as my brother, and your daughter will become our niece."

Michael didn't know what to say. Although he believed this man, all he wanted was to return home to the Mohan camp with Mary. Correctly reading Michael's thoughts, Simon spoke softly to Michael. "Smile and nod your head yes."

There are worse fates than being the adopted brother of the chief, thought Michael. He managed a smile, put his hand out to the chief, and Red Hawk, who had experience with the white man's ways, shook Michael's hand.

Everyone agreed. Tomorrow they would have the adoption ceremony, and there would be a great feast. In the meantime, Michael just wanted to rest, hold his daughter, and figure out a way to get out of this village and return to the Mohans. It would not be easy. Although the tribe was planning to adopt him, Michael knew there were some here who would not hesitate to kill him, and Mary, too. He would play along with them until he could win their trust and then try to escape.

Mary and White Feather were talking to each other as if they were kin. She needed a female influence, and who better than the wife of the chief. Michael knew that if the chief and his wife were evil people, Mary would know and not be so friendly. He also knew that his daughter would be more interested in what the young braves were learning than how to be a good Shawnee girl. She already had skills not normally of interest to a young girl. Michael made a mental note to talk to Simon Girty about this; he did not want any trouble.

Red Hawk and White Feather left, and two women remained to make sure Michael and Mary ate something and were comfortable for the night. Michael didn't have to look outside to know there was a warrior guarding their wigwam. Michael closed his eyes and it seemed like only a minute passed before he was again dreaming of his beloved wife and the green hills of Ireland.

Chapter 10

THE FEAST

May 1763

Mary was up and awake at dawn. She was excited about the special ceremony today. Michael was still very tired and sore, although the ointments the women had rubbed him with the previous evening seemed to have helped.

Simon Girty was the first to arrive at the wigwam, followed by the same two women who had brought food and tended to Michael the day before. Simon explained what would happen later in the day, how the adoption ceremony would go, and that there would be drumming and feasting lasting into the night. He explained to Michael what a great honor it was to be adopted by the chief. Simon was concerned that Michael would not take this adoption seriously, that he would run at the first chance, but Michael assured him he knew the importance of the ceremony without Simon going into great detail.

Michael thanked his new friend and assured him that he wasn't going anywhere. Simon and Michael both knew this meant he wasn't in any shape physically to accomplish a getaway, not now anyway. Michael was glad for Simon's concern; he wouldn't be alive if he hadn't interceded in his behalf.

The village was full of activity: the women were cooking, and the warriors seemed excited about the upcoming ceremony and were preparing their large drum for the evening celebration.

Michael had five minutes alone with his daughter, during which time he explained what was going to happen. "There will be an adoption ceremony, making me Chief Red Hawk's brother. We will eat with Chief Red Hawk and his wife, White Feather, and the entire village. Afterwards, there will be drumming, singing, and dancing." Seeing the worried look on Mary's face, Michael hugged her and asked, "What's wrong, Mary?"

"Does this mean we will stay here forever and not go back to the Mohans' camp?"

Michael wasn't sure from his daughter's question or her demeanor which one she preferred. "What do you want to do?"

"I like it here. Chief Red Hawk and White Feather are strong and brave people, and we could learn much from them."

Michael took a long time to answer his daughter. "It looks like we will be staying here, Mary. After all, I will become the chief's brother and you his niece."

Mary smiled at her father, hugged him, and then went out of the wigwam.

Michael had mixed feelings about what he had told his daughter. He too liked Red Hawk and White Feather. He had made a friend in Simon Girty. The warriors accepted them and respected Michael for his efforts during the gauntlet. His main concern was Snapping Turtle, who he knew didn't share the other warriors' respect for him. Michael would have to keep his guard up and be prepared for anything.

He left the wigwam and searched the area for Mary. He would have to keep her in his sight unless she was with Red Hawk or

White Feather. He found her in the center of the village with the women who were preparing the feast. Michael walked over to them and asked Mary if she was helping.

One of the women, Willow, smiled and answered for Mary. She understood and spoke English and had already started to teach the young girl the Shawnee language. "Your daughter is going to be a fine young lady and will make a good wife for one of the warriors."

Michael tried not to change his expression as he answered, "Thank you." The thought of Mary with any man, let alone one of these warriors, made his skin crawl. He knew he would face that someday, he just didn't want to think of it now, especially knowing the brutality these people were capable of.

Michael would eventually find that both the white man and the red man were capable of atrocious acts of violence and incredible loving deeds.

Chief Red Hawk appeared and asked Michael if he was ready for the ceremony, and Michael replied, "Yes. Can Mary be there too?"

"Yes, of course," said Red Hawk. "I need you to come to my lodge so that you will have something of mine to wear. Bring Mary. White Feather has something for her to wear."

With that, the three walked to the chief's lodge. It was warm and comfortable. White Feather smiled as they entered, and the red-haired girl quickly ran to her. White Feather pulled an outfit from her belongings and held it up to Mary.

As Mary changed into her new regalia, Red Hawk handed Michael a beautiful, beaded elk-hide shirt with matching leggings.

His wife had made them for him a couple of years before but had since made him new ones. Red Hawk also gave Michael a breech-cloth to complete the outfit and motioned for Michael to put everything on. The chief's generosity overwhelmed Michael. Since Mary was now dressed in her new outfit, White Feather said she would take her to show the other women so Michael could change.

Michael stepped out of the chief's lodge, and as he did, the other warriors quickly surrounded him. Red Wing, also a chief, was the first to place his hand on Michael's shoulder. He explained that he would be performing the adoption ceremony. Red Hawk stood to Michael's left, Red Wing to Michael's right, and the three men walked to the center of the village. The rest of the warriors followed behind, except for Snapping Turtle. Michael did not see him in the group of warriors.

The villagers made a circle with the three men in the middle by the fire. Red Wing formally asked, "Who will be adopted today?"

Michael answered, "I will be adopted."

Red Wing then asked, "Who will adopt this man?"

Red Hawk answered, "I will adopt this man."

Red Wing mixed water and earth and asked Michael if he could separate the water and earth he had joined.

Michael answered, "No."

Red Wing then placed the mixed water and earth on Red Hawk's forehead, then Michael's, and said, "As the water and earth that I have placed on your foreheads cannot be separated, neither can you be separated. Now you are one. Now you are the same for life."

Michael wasn't sure what to do next. Red Hawk reached out for him, and Michael and the chief hugged. "Now we are brothers!" the chief announced.

The villagers let out loud cheers, and each warrior came to Michael to welcome him into the tribe. Except one. Michael wouldn't let himself think about that one person now. He felt closer to this man Red Hawk than he ever had to his older brother, John Ryan.

The women made sure everyone ate their fill, and the drumming began. White Feather took Mary's hand and showed her how to dance to the drumbeats. Michael, caught up in the moment, followed Red Hawk around the drum and felt a kinship to this red man who had taken him as his brother.

After a couple of hours, the celebration ended. Again, the warriors came to Michael and put their hands on his muscled shoulders as they welcomed him and Mary to their tribe. When Michael tried to give back his regalia, Red Hawk put his right hand up and said, "No. They are yours, my brother!"

Mary said goodnight to her new aunt and uncle and walked with her father to their wigwam. They both were tired, but the love shown to them tonight was powerful. Michael quickly kissed his daughter, and they both snuggled into their beds to sleep. Michael noticed this was the first night that a warrior did not stand guard outside their wigwam. Sleep came quickly to both father and daughter.

It wasn't long before both Michael and Mary became accustomed to their new family and their different way of life. Both were learning the Shawnee language, Michael was a great shot and contributed to the meat for camp as much as the other warriors did, and Mary was learning about edible plants, natural medicines, and how to prepare the wild game the warriors brought in.

As much as Michael felt a closeness to his new brother and his wife, he couldn't shake the feeling that he needed to get back to the Mohans' camp. The British were not allowing settlements west of the Appalachian Mountains, but few settlers listened. Some of the Indians tried to remain neutral, but the British kept pushing them to fight against the encroaching settlers. It was not a peaceful time to be on the frontier. Michael was afraid of what might happen to them if white men attacked this village.

It wouldn't be long before the decision was made for him.

Chapter 11

CHIEF PONTIAC

1763 - 1766

Simon Girty did not want to bring up anything negative during the celebration when his new friend, Michael, was adopted by Red Hawk, but there were many things weighing on his mind. The Eastern tribes accepted Girty, and he was privilege to information from different sources. The following day, Girty met with Red Hawk and Red Wing to let them know what he had heard.

It was common knowledge among the tribes that the French and British had fought against each other to control this land since they both had arrived in North America. Many of the native tribes had sided with the French at the beginning of the French and Indian War, which was part of the worldwide Seven Years War.

Girty related to the two chiefs the concerns some of the Eastern tribes had about the current situation between the French and their Indian allies. Early in the fighting in the Ohio River Valley, the French had control of Fort Duquesne, their main base of operation. It sat on the strategic site where the Allegheny and Monongahela rivers joined to form the Ohio River. General John Forbes planned to capture the fort, but his success was dependent on separating the French from their Native American allies. He sent Moravian missionaries, who were on good terms with the Native Americans, to offer them a deal: if the Indians would abandon the French, the British, after winning the war, would return their lands, withdraw troops, and allow no white settlement west of the Allegheny Mountains. The Iroquois, or Six Nations, the Shawnee, and the Delaware accepted the offer; they were tired of fighting.

The French could not defend Fort Duquesne without their Indian allies. They destroyed it and abandoned the area in 1758. The British occupied the area and started to build Fort Pitt. This became the British center of operations in the west for years to come. The loss of Fort Duquesne was the beginning of the end for the French. They were too broke to continue the fight and ceased hostilities in North America.

The British did not keep their promises to return the lands to the Indians; instead, they remained on the lands and built forts while settlers continued their push westward. They made no attempt to establish a rapport with the native tribes, something the French had done effectively. Tensions ran high as the Indians watched the influx of more whites. The amount of goods available to the Indians at trading posts was much less than it had been. The British instituted trade rules forbidding the sale of powder and bullets to the Indians but allowed the sale of alcohol. The British also violated previous treaties with the natives by building forts in the Ohio country. They had promised to stop the influx of settlers across the Allegheny Mountains but did not enforce it. The American frontier once again erupted in violence.

Pontiac, chief of the Ottawa tribe, had been a staunch supporter of the French, and when the British began taking over New France, he began urging violent resistance against them. Girty reported that the tribal leaders in the Great Lakes region were aligning themselves with Pontiac and had joined him in attacking forts, settlements, and homesteads. The Indians had attacked several forts in the past few months, including the siege of Fort Detroit, led by Pontiac. Because the warriors surrounded the fort, the troops were trapped inside the fort while Pontiac's warriors killed everyone in the surrounding countryside except for a few French settlers. The Indians wanted to drive out the other white settlers. That was their goal.

According to Girty, the British considered the uprising to be a local problem—until Fort Pitt became a target. Red Hawk and Walking Owl explained that they did not send warriors to attack Fort Pitt—they still believed negotiations were possible—but Simon confirmed that was not the case. Delegations of Shawnee, Ottawa, and Delaware tried to convince Alexander McKee and Captain Simeon Ecuyer, the commander of Fort Pitt, that they should leave the fort before many large numbers of Indians arrived to attack it, but to no avail. A force of 500 Indians attacked Fort Pitt on May 29, 1763. The people defending the fort managed to fend off the attack, but the Indians laid siege to it, cutting supply and reinforcement lines, like they had at Fort Detroit. They raided areas in western Pennsylvania, western Maryland, and down into Virginia.

Prior to the siege, Captain Ecuyer got a message through to Fort Ligonier, detailing his situation. Fort Ligonier was forty miles to the east and had been under attack twice in June. The siege of Fort Pitt continued without let up through June and July. Over 1,500 people were sheltered inside the fort, food was running out, and smallpox was a problem.

Red Hawk and Walking Owl agreed to send some warriors to Fort Pitt to help in the fighting. They could not send all of their warriors, but Red Wing could take a group from both villages to, hopefully, put an end to the siege and fighting in the Ohio Valley.

During the last week of July, the Indians, including the warriors with Red Wing, attacked from all directions, firing non-stop day and night. They tried to dig, burn, or chop their way into the fort. For five days the defenders of Fort Pitt dropped hot liquids, grenades, whatever they could find, on the attackers. On August 1, the siege lifted. Captain Ecuyer figured a relief force must be on the way. Assigned to lead the relief expedition to Fort Pitt was Colonel Henry Bouquet. The Indians moved on to intercept Bouquet and his men.

Colonel Henry Bouquet had been General Forbes' second-in-command. He understood frontier warfare and had skillfully trained his men in it. Bouquet and his forces reached Fort Ligonier on August 2. They left for Fort Pitt on August 4 with a total of 400 men. Their halfway destination was Bushy Run Station, which had good water and forage for the livestock.

It was at Bushy Run that Colonel Bouquet met the Indians who had left the siege at Fort Pitt to do battle with him.

Girty explained that some of the tribes had signed many treaties in the last couple of years, although Chief Pontiac did not sign a peace treaty officially ending his war until 1766. The three men discussed how much support Pontiac had from many tribes in the beginning, but his influence among his followers had waned. They agreed life as they had known it was changing, and they were afraid they would never get their lands back or drive the white man from their tribal homelands.

In 1768 Pontiac left his Ottawa village on the Maumee River and relocated near Ouiatenon on the Wabash River. He was increasingly ostracized and eventually assassinated by a Peoria warrior in 1769.

Chapter 12

MAMA BEAR

July 1763

As Mary and her father traveled through the woods with her adopted uncle and aunt, Red Hawk and White Feather, the young girl could not help but notice all the beautiful wonders surrounding her: the wildflowers were in full bloom, the squirrels played and chattered in the trees above, and sunlight filtered through the leaves, making the trail look as if it were part of another world. Mary loved being in the woods and loved the plants and animals. She was quiet as they made their way to the next village. They were going to the village where Walking Owl lived. He was Red Hawk's brother, a chief also and a medicine man.

Suddenly, a feeling came over Mary, a bad feeling that made the hair on the back of her neck stand up and sent cold chills down her spine. She knew this feeling; she had felt it before on the day the Shawnee warriors took her and her father captive. Mary saw a picture in her head, a picture of a large black bear mauling her beloved uncle.

"Uncle," Mary cried out. "Stop!"

Red Hawk had also been enjoying the warm day, and his thoughts were on the upcoming gathering. He stopped on the trail, turning back to her, and saw Mary, in tears, running towards him.

"Uncle, you must take us from this place. There is a large bear nearby and she will kill you if we don't turn around!"

Red Hawk had come to know this girl and love her. But he was still getting used to her telling him things before they happened, and he did not want to delay their arrival at his brother's village. "Mary," he said quietly, "there are no bears around here, we will be safe. I promise to be careful. We will be there soon."

Mary was insistent, and her father knew she would not give up until Red Hawk had done as she asked. Michael asked, "Couldn't we take a different trail, one that would maybe get us there a little later, but would make Mary happy?"

Before Red Hawk could answer, Mary let out a scream that would have woken the dead. Before the adults could stop her, she took off to the right of the trail. The men both followed her through the bushes into a small clearing where they saw a mother black bear and her cub. Mary was yelling at the bear to leave. Michael had just reached for her to pull her back when the mother bear charged right for Red Hawk. Both men pulled their knives, and when Michael did, he let go of Mary. Mary ran closer to the bear, and this time talked quietly to her. "Please, mama, we mean you no harm. Take your baby and go. We won't hurt either of you."

By this time White Feather had joined them in the clearing. All three adults watched in disbelief as the large black bear looked at them, then Mary, and then moved through the bushes away from them, her cub following. All four people stood still for a moment, catching their breath before anyone spoke.

Michael's first instinct was to chastise his daughter for running toward the bear, but before he could speak, Red Hawk knelt and spoke to Mary. "Thank you, my child, for saving me from the bear." He had tears in his eyes as he pulled Mary close to him and gave thanks to the Creator for bringing her into their lives. He knew she had a gift for talking to the animals, as well as other gifts that were difficult to understand, but he also knew she had a purpose, a destiny that she must fulfill.

Mary also had tears in her eyes for she knew she had disobeyed her father, but she was fearless when it came to protecting the ones she loved. "You are welcome, Uncle! We can go now."

The group moved on toward the village of Red Hawk's brother, Walking Owl, who was expecting them before sundown for the gathering. No one spoke about the bear, Mary, or the fact that she had persuaded the mama bear to leave. All three adults knew that a mother bear could be dangerous, and especially vicious when protecting her cub, but they also knew that Mary was capable of things they could not explain.

Chapter 13

WALKING OWL

July 1763

Walking Owl had been expecting the arrival of his brother, Red Hawk, his wife, White Feather, the white man Red Hawk had recently adopted, and the white man's daughter. Walking Owl's brother had never adopted a captive before, and he wondered what was so special about this man. He would soon find out.

The villagers were also expecting the arrival of the chief's brother, his wife, and their white captives now accepted as blood relatives. Tensions had been high between the Indians and the whites who continued their unending influx into the area. Local natives attacked forts, and settlers were being killed or burned out. It was difficult to imagine a good relationship between the two races. Walking Owl respected his brother, though, so if Red Hawk felt this man was worthy to be a Shawnee, then he, Walking Owl, must do everything he could to make this man and his daughter welcome and control his warriors, who could sometimes go against his wishes.

The four travelers were at once surrounded as they entered the village. At first Michael felt threatened by the pressing crowd. It reminded him of the day he and Mary entered Red Hawk's village and the warriors threatened to burn him at the stake. Mary, on the other hand, had a huge smile on her face. Everyone made a special effort to make them feel at home. Of course, Mary's bright auburn hair made her the center of attention.

After Walking Owl welcomed them, he took them to the wigwam they would share during their visit. After settling in, the four made their way to the center of the village where the women had been working on the evening meal.

When the villagers were seated, Red Hawk stood up to introduce his new brother. He explained how they had come to be a part of his family, touching lightly on the fact that Michael had been responsible for a warrior's death. He explained that Michael had run the gauntlet, and he described the unforgettable ending to his run. Then the chief focused on young Mary. No sound came from the villagers as he described the encounter with the she-bear on the way to his brother's village. Mary started to blush, then wrapped her arms around Red Hawk's neck as he picked her up. "This young lady saved my life." Red Hawk was obviously very fond of Mary and Michael, and so was White Feather. Everyone cheered.

Walking Owl approached his brother, touched Mary on her shoulder, and said, "Thank you." He then stepped over to where Michael was sitting, and Michael stood up to face him. Walking Owl said, "Welcome, both of you, into our family. Thank you for bringing this young woman to us. May you both live long and happy lives." The two men embraced, both thinking of the turmoil going on outside the village between their two races.

Michael had come to realize that not all Indians were cruel savages, just as he had learned that not all white men were without fault. He wished that he could help bring the two sides together, to help heal the hurt done by both.

Walking Owl talked with Michael and Mary during the meal. After hearing what his brother had said about Mary saving his life, the chief centered his attention on the young girl. He soon realized that she was beyond her years in wisdom and had unique qualities normally associated with elders or medicine men.

Walking Owl asked, "How did you know the mama bear was near the trail?"

Mary was slow to answer. Sometimes, she was not sure herself how she knew things—she just knew them. "I saw her in my mind," the young girl answered.

"My brother says that you talk to the animals. How did you learn their languages?"

"I just hear their voices in my head."

Walking Owl was quiet for a time. Finally, he looked at Mary and said, "You have a purpose in this life. It is up to you to find out what that is, I cannot tell you. You must seek the answers yourself." Mary listened quietly, without speaking, as the chief continued. "There are special plans for you."

Mary had a questioning look on her face but again she did not speak.

"These are not my plans, but I can tell you that no man shall walk in front of you—you will walk first."

Mary smiled as if she understood.

This would be the first of many conversations between Walking Owl and Mary, as they would speak frequently over the next few years. She would learn from him, and he from her.

Chapter 14

JOHN "CROW" RYAN

August 1763

John Ryan hated Indians. He had taken an oath while kneeling beside his son's grave to spend the rest of his life killing them, and he did. He had lived with his wife, son, and daughter near Winchester, Virginia. In August 1763 five Indians captured sixteen-year-old Eleanor Ryan and her eleven-year-old brother, John. They killed and scalped his wife and burned his house and all his belongings. The children, riding on stolen horses led by the Indians into the western mountains, were taken to some Indian town on the Ohio River.

The warriors first took the children to the Cacapon River. A scouting party came near them, causing alarm among the Indians. Three of the warriors approached the rear of the scouting party with their flintlocks cocked, ready to fire. The other two stayed by their captives with their tomahawks raised, ready to strike them if they made any noise to warn the white men. The Indians saw that the party had too many men for them to fight, so they remained quiet and let them pass. After seeing signs of other scouting parties, the Indians changed their course to go through the most rugged moun-tains they could find to prevent the whites from tracking them. The warriors weren't in a hurry, though, and did some hunting and fishing along the way. Two weeks after their capture, the young boy and his sister arrived at the upper forks of the Monongahela, at the confluence of the Tygart Valley and West Fork rivers.

Since they were quite exhausted and unable to go much farther, Eleanor and her brother expected they would be murdered soon by the warriors, as most captives were who became too ill or unable to travel. They decided to try to escape. That night, as they had done every night since their capture, the children looked for firewood. After making three trips back into camp, they went out once more, but this time they hid themselves in a laurel thicket until the Indians gave up looking for them.

For three weeks the siblings wandered about in the wilderness, following different paths eastward during daylight but often losing their direction, causing them to travel mostly in circles. Young John became ill and eventually died. Eleanor was asleep when her brother died. She awoke to the grizzly site of six buzzards walking on a log, leaving bloody tracks. After looking behind the log, Eleanor saw four of the birds perched on young John's body, ripping at his flesh. It was more than the young girl could bear. She thrashed about, striking at the birds, trying to get them away from her brother. She was crazy with the pain of losing him. She had been through so much these last few weeks, and now she lost all track of time as she ran about gathering stones to cover John's body. She hadn't eaten in several days and was close to death herself. But even in her deteriorated state, Eleanor had the presence of mind to mark the site of her brother's grave by stripping limbs from small trees nearby.

The next day she found the remains of a deer with a little meat hanging on the bones that she quickly devoured. It was the first food she had eaten since her escape except for two roots and a bite of turtle flesh she had found. Later that day she found a well-worn path leading eastward, which she followed for a week. During this time she was not aware of her actions, sometimes finding herself on her knees or lying down, crying or mumbling prayers. It was growing dark when she found herself in a clearing and saw a stockade in front of her. She fainted, and when she came to, she was lying in a bed in a cabin at Fort Harness on the south branch of the Potomac River.

John Ryan visited what is now Marion County in the fall of 1763 in hopes of finding his son's body and giving it a proper burial. John Ice led Ryan to his son's grave on White Day Creek, near the mouth of Cherry Run, where John Beall and John Ice had found young John Ryan's body a few weeks before and buried him.

After Ryan made his oath to kill any Indian he saw, John Ice tried to lighten the mood by informing him that a man named Michael Ryan had mentioned he had a brother named John. Both he and his daughter were staying at Mohan's Camp, not far away. Michael had come to Virginia in hopes of finding his brother.

John Ryan did not seem to hear Ice at first. He was still caught up in his emotions and the thoughts of his son's death. When he did answer, it was more of a growl. "What's that you say? Michael is here?"

"So you do have a brother named Michael," Ice replied. "If you want to accompany me to Mohan's Camp, you can rest up before you leave."

John Ryan did not have any specific plans except to kill every Indian he found. His daughter was with his wife's sister in Winchester, and Ryan was not expected to return there anytime soon. It had been years since he had seen Michael; they had never really been close. John was older than Michael and had left their homeland years before Michael and Mary left. He had nothing to lose by checking this man out to see if they were related. If they were, hopefully, this Ryan would help him kill Indians.

The trip to Mohan's Camp proved to be a waste of time. John Mohan told the elder Ryan brother that his brother and niece were captives of the Shawnee. This further angered the Irishman; now he had even more reason to hate the red man!

Little did John Ryan or his brother, Michael, know that John would come to be known as Indian Killer Ryan as he killed Indians up and down the Monongahela and Ohio valleys, westward into Illinois, and southward into Kentucky. Both John and Michael Ryan were just beginning their associations with the native people, whether good or bad, and it would forever change both their lives.

Chapter 15

BATTLE OF BUSHY RUN

August 1763

Combined forces of Delaware, Shawnee, Mingo, and Huron warriors laid siege to Fort Pitt in the summer of 1763. During the last week of July, the Indians, including the warriors with Red Wing, attacked from all directions, firing non-stop day and night. They tried to dig, burn, or chop their way in. For five days the defenders of Fort Pitt dropped hot liquids, grenades, whatever they could find, on their attackers. On August 1, the siege lifted. Captain Ecuyer figured a relief force must be on the way. Assigned to lead the relief expedition to Fort Pitt was Colonel Henry Bouquet. The Indians moved on to intercept Bouquet and his men.

Colonel Henry Bouquet, an experienced wilderness fighter, was a Swiss national who had seen action in Europe before joining the British Army and coming to fight in America. His force consisted of tough men experienced in battle. A large number of them were Scottish Highlanders from the 42nd (Black Watch) Regiment and the 77th (Montgomerie's Highlanders) Regiment. There were also men from the 60th (Royal American) Regiment. Instead of swords, they all carried tomahawks or hatchets.

Bouquet's relief force left Fort Ligonier on August 4, 1763. They marched twelve miles that day and made encampment along the road. The next day they marched twenty more miles in the heat. By 1:00 p.m., the head of the column was only a mile from Bushy

Run Station. As they entered a gully between two hills, the Indians opened fire. Although his men did as they had been trained—advance into the trees to engage their attackers—the Indians simply were not there. They had moved unseen through the trees along both sides of the column.

Bouquet ordered a fighting retreat, planning to reach the lightly defended pack train they could not afford to lose to the Indians. The Indians, however, remained in the trees and were not lured out into the open by their enemy. Bouquet's men built a circular stockade using hundreds of meal bags that had been tied to the pack horses. This became known as the "flour bag fort." The supplies, livestock, and wounded men were crammed inside.

The fighting lasted for hours. As darkness overtook the forest, the night was full of cries of the wounded, nervous animals and spine-tingling Indian war whoops. Fighting started again at daybreak. The Indians were closing in on the British, whose casualties continued to rise. Bouquet, knowing it was common for Indians to leave defenders an escape route, sent two companies over the hill to the east, as if they were retreating. The plan was to draw the Indians out in the open, and it worked. The two companies who had gone over the hill turned and began attacking the Indians from the right. Two more companies charged down the hill, causing the Indians to run.

During this time, a woman, obviously a warrior, appeared out of nowhere. She stood over six feet tall, was painted in war paint, and was naked to the waist. The whites had never seen anything like her. They would find out later her name was Nonhelema. She was the sister of Cornstalk, and she and her brother were both Shawnee chiefs. People called her the Grenadier or Grenadier Squaw because of her height. She would play a part in the history of this area for years.

Bouquet won the Battle of Bushy Run and saved Fort Pitt, ending Pontiac's War. It had been costly though. There were fifty dead, sixty wounded, and five soldiers missing. The force was short on horses and water and exhausted from three days of non-stop marching and fighting. Supplies that couldn't be carried were burned, and soldiers killed the injured animals. There were no wagons, so the soldiers made stretchers for the wounded.

Burial parties gathered the dead soldiers and buried them in a mass grave on top of the ridge where the Indians had ambushed them. Then the group moved towards Bushy Run Station, where they would stay until August 8th.

Bouquet's forces covered twenty-six miles in three days, fully expecting the Indians to attack again at any moment. But the trip to Fort Pitt was uneventful, and they arrived on August 10th to find the Union Jack still flying. Although the threat of Indian attacks was still there, the Indian menace in the immediate area had been stopped for now.

Red Wing and the surviving warriors who accompanied him returned to Red Hawk and Walking Owl and reported their defeat at Bushy Run. The Indians began to realize they could not afford to lose forty to fifty braves in every battle. There just were not that many of them to begin with. But the whites had almost unlimited manpower. There were approximately 50,000 Native Americans living in the region, 10,000 of them warriors. The European colonists numbered over a million, with more arriving every day. The

Indians began avoiding major engagements and tried to negotiate better deals while they could.

Although the war picked up again in the spring, it was in the form of isolated raids. A reinforced and more aggressive British army had the tribes on the run. Colonel Bouquet commanded the last British foray in October of 1764. He led 1,500 men to the junction of the Muskingum and Tuscarawas Rivers, 120 miles due west of Fort Pitt. Instead of attacking the Indians, he sent an offer to parlay. Bouquet secured the release of hundreds of white captives and negotiated a truce with the Indians—all without firing a single shot. According to the Articles of Agreement of November 1764, the Delaware and Shawnee tribes would cease hostilities against all British subjects and release all English prisoners, deserters, Frenchmen, Negroes, and any other white people living among them. Red Hawk was one of many Shawnee chiefs who reluctantly agreed to return their captives. It would take another twenty months of negotiations before a formal peace treaty officially ended the war in July 1766.

Bushy Run marked the beginning of the end for the Native American's way of life and opened the possibilities of western migration and settlement. Within ten years, western Pennsylvania was no longer the frontier. The British abandoned Fort Ligonier in 1766 and sold Fort Pitt to two colonists in 1772.

Among the white captives returned to Bouquet were William Ice, John Ice, Thomas Ice, Elizabeth Ice, Michael Ryan, his daughter, Mary, and Joseph Studebaker.

Chapter 16

JOSEPH STUDEBAKER

1764

Colonel Bouquet's forces took 194 captives from the Delawares in October and November of 1764. One of them was Joseph Studebaker, who explained to the colonel the circumstances of his capture.

On March 3, 1756, a band of Delaware Indians led by Captain Jacobs and Chief Shingas raided the Studebaker farm, south of Welsh Run Creek in southern Pennsylvania. Heinrich Studebaker and his son Joseph were clearing stumps from their field. A warrior killed Heinrich before he could reach his gun. Another grabbed young Joseph as he tried to run. The mother and three of her children, Joseph, Phillip, and Elizabeth, became hostages of the Delaware. The oldest child, Susannah, was visiting family nearby.

The Indians looted the cabin then pushed the family to hurry along the paths. It was during the march to the Delaware village at Kittanning that the warriors killed Joseph's mother and her unborn baby. When the three Studebaker children reached the village, the women took them to the Allegheny River, where they washed the white blood out of their bodies; this was part of the adoption ceremony into the tribe.

Young Joseph was responsible for entering a cave containing a hibernating bear and driving it outside for the men to kill. While the Studebaker children were learning the ways of their captors, the colonies and French waged war around them.

Lieutenant Colonel John Armstrong led an attack on Kittanning. On the morning of September 8, 1756, just six months after the raid on the Studebaker farm, Armstrong and his forces took the Delaware village by surprise. The children hid in a nearby cornfield while the fighting continued. Armstrong ordered the burning of the Delaware houses. Captain Jacobs, his wife, and son were killed before they could escape. Eleven captives were freed from Kittanning, although four died during the flight from the village. Other captives, including the Studebaker children, were taken west. The children were separated after fleeing Kittanning, but they continued to live with the Delaware for several years.

Philip Studebaker returned to his family in 1762. Joseph Studebaker and his sister Elizabeth were to be returned to waiting family in Carlisle in 1764, after Colonel Bouquet's demand that the white captives be returned. Joseph returned, reluctantly, but Elizabeth and Rhody Boyd, another captive, escaped and returned to the Delaware.

Joseph wanted to return to his Delaware father, but his family had a party and invited local young ladies. One of them, Molly Teeter, caught Joseph's eye. Joseph married Molly and began raising a family. He took part in the Revolutionary War, serving under General Washington. It wasn't until his family was grown that he finally moved back to the area of western Pennsylvania where he had spent time with the Delaware.

Chapter 17

SNAPPING TURTLE

October 1764

Life in the Shawnee village of Red Hawk and his wife, White Feather, was not difficult for Michael Ryan and his daughter except for one thing—the intense hatred Snapping Turtle and now, his son, Digging Turtle, had for them. Michael had killed Running Badger, Snapping Turtle's brother. Digging Turtle was now old enough to be a warrior and was trying to prove himself worthy. He became enraged when young Mary beat him not only in a foot race but also with her skills with a bow and arrow. Michael was always alert for any negative behavior from the father and son. He cautioned Mary to be aware of her surroundings and not let herself be alone with either one.

The situation became worse after the Battle of Bushy Run. Warriors from the village took part in the battle. Chief Red Hawk did not expect Michael to join the fighting; he understood it would create difficulty for Michael in the future if it were known that he fought against his own people. Red Hawk was an understanding leader and tried to do what was good for all his people, but there were warriors who did not agree with his decision to let Michael stay in the village instead of fighting. Even though Red Hawk explained that Michael was left behind to help protect the village, Snapping Turtle took every opportunity to make life unpleasant for Michael and Mary. Now his son was focusing on young Mary, and

Michael knew it was just a matter of time before there was a confrontation between the two fathers.

Snapping Turtle was a warrior, but he was not an honorable one like Red Hawk. He was sneaky. In front of his chief, he pretended to go along with accepting the adopted whites into their village, but when given the opportunity, he would make comments under his breath, criticizing Michael, his abilities as a warrior, and threatening him and his daughter. The situation was a powder keg just waiting for the fuse to be lit.

It happened during a hunt in the fall of 1774. Several warriors, including Snapping Turtle, Digging Turtle, White Bear, and Michael, were three miles from their village. Red Hawk had chosen to stay in the village, as he had to figure out what he was going to do about the agreement he made with Colonel Bouquet to give back all white captives. Red Hawk had an uneasy feeling about the hunting party because he knew Snapping Turtle still had a vendetta against his white brother, Michael.

He was confident that White Bear could manage the situation, until Mary came running to him with the same look on her face she'd had when they confronted the mother bear. "Uncle, please! My father is in grave danger. Snapping Turtle is going to kill him!"

Red Hawk knew better than to question her, as she had proven herself before in the last few months. "Do not worry, I will go myself to check on them," was his reply. He quickly called on Red Wing, and the two of them set out for the area where they knew the warriors would be.

They were too late. Snapping Turtle had planned to get Michael alone, kill him, and then say Michael had attacked him. What he did not count on was the strength the Irishman had, mentally and physically. Michael was not an easy target. As the party fanned out in search of deer, Michael tried to stay close to White Bear, knowing Snapping Turtle would antagonize him every chance he got. Michael saw a large buck ahead of him and readied his arrow to send it flying into the side of the buck.

Just as he drew back his bow, he heard a noise to his left. Snapping Turtle was so focused on his goal—killing Michael Ryan—that he wasn't taking the time to place his feet on the forest floor so as not to make any noise. In addition, his son, Digging Turtle, was also in a hurry to make the white man pay.

Michael turned his attention toward the noise and saw father and son, both with knives drawn, coming at him with hatred in their eyes. Michael's arrow was nocked on his bow string, so he let it fly. Unfortunately for Digging Turtle, it was aimed toward his left shoulder. The arrow struck its target, stopping the young man in his tracks. He let out a scream that the other hunters heard, and they came running. This enraged Snapping Turtle to the point that he didn't bother to stop to check his son but continued on his hell-bent rage to kill Michael.

Anger consumed the Shawnee man. He wasn't thinking clearly and was blindly thrusting his knife toward Michael, who analyzed the situation correctly and fought a defensive fight. Michael was able to cut Snapping Turtle's arms, along with throwing a couple of punches when an opportunity presented itself. Michael received a couple of small cuts but nothing like his opponent. Snapping Turtle made one last attempt to thrust his knife into Michael's chest, but

Michael pushed the man's arm away with his left hand and, with his right hand, thrust his knife into Snapping Turtle's upper abdomen, stopping the fight.

Most of the other warriors had come running from the woods at the same time. They could see there had been a fight, and knowing the circumstances between the two men, they didn't have to be told who had started it. Red Hawk and Red Wing arrived a couple of minutes later, only to see Snapping Turtle dead on the ground, covered in blood, and his son, Digging Turtle, with an arrow in his shoulder.

The warriors tended to the young man the best they could, and the party started back toward their village with Snapping Turtle's body tied to a horse and Digging Turtle riding behind one of the warriors. The young man was almost delirious with pain and unaware that his father was dead.

Red Hawk walked with Michael for five minutes without saying anything. When he spoke, it was with great sadness. "My brother, I am sorry that you had to endure this from one of my warriors. I should have never let the two of you join in this hunt together. I wasn't thinking clearly."

Michael was also slow to reply. "Red Hawk," he finally said, "it is not your fault. It was bound to happen. I killed his brother and he wanted revenge."

Both men were thinking about the same possible event in the future—when Digging Turtle would seek his revenge—but neither spoke of it. Instead, Red Hawk told Michael of the agreement that stated the Shawnee had to return any white captives. He hated to do it, but he had no choice. The two men had become brothers since the adoption ceremony, and the entire village—except for a couple of warriors—had accepted Michael and Mary as their own. But both Red Hawk and Michael knew there was no other choice: father and daughter would return to Mohan's Camp as soon as possible. Michael didn't want to cause his brother any trouble with Colonel Bouquet, and if they left the village, maybe Digging Turtle wouldn't be reminded of his father's death as much without Michael there to remind him.

Within three months, Colonel Bouquet would ride into the Indian village and take Michael Ryan and Mary back to Mohan's Camp.

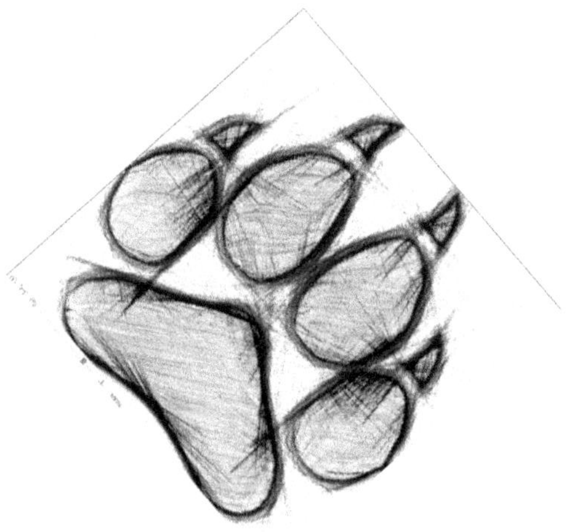

Chapter 18

RETURN TO MOHAN'S CAMP

January 1765

The journey with Colonel Bouquet was bittersweet for both Michael and Mary. They had genuinely loved Red Hawk, White Feather, and the Shawnee of their village, and both hated to leave them. The unpleasant memories of Snapping Turtle and Digging Turtle balanced their reluctance to leave, each knowing it was good to put some distance between them and the evil son.

During their trip, they met others who were also captive and were returning home, some from the same area where they had been taken, others going to Pennsylvania. Two of the former captives they met were Joseph Studebaker and his sister Elizabeth. Michael enjoyed talking with the young man. Joseph too had not wanted to leave his Delaware Indian father but had no choice. His tales of their capture sent chills down Michael's spine. The Delaware had killed both parents and adopted the three children, who had lived with them for many years.

The two men shook hands when they parted, and Elizabeth hugged Mary. The Studebakers would be delivered to Carlisle, Pennsylvania. Michael, Mary, and other captives from Augusta, Virginia, arrived at Fort Pitt on January 5, 1765.

As Michael and Mary made their way south to Mohan's Camp from Fort Pitt, Michael reflected on the last year and a half. He thought of the day Mary had interrupted the hunting trip, and of being taken captive by the three Shawnee warriors, running the gauntlet, and later becoming the brother of Chief Red Hawk. Michael and Mary had become very close to the chief and his wife, White Feather, and they hated to leave them but knew there was no other choice. Between Colonel Bouquet's efforts to free captives and the difficult situation between Michael, Snapping Turtle, and Digging Turtle, there was no other choice but to return to the Mohan brothers. Hopefully, Red Hawk and White Feather could visit them at Mohan's Camp, Michael thought. At least they would be welcome there.

Michael was sure the Mohans had held his cabin for him. He couldn't wait to get there, settle in, and resume his life in the white man's world. Mary was unusually quiet on the trip and Michael knew she was missing Red Hawk and White Feather.

When Michael and Mary walked into Mohan's Camp, the Mohans greeted them with cheers, hugs, and a warm meal. The brothers were expecting their release and were hoping the Ryans would return to them. There were many questions about their capture, their time with the Shawnee, and how it felt to be home again.

Michael explained how the Shawnee warriors had surprised them and how he had killed one of the warriors and wounded the other two. No one in the camp was surprised that Mary bandaged all of the wounded and hid all the weapons. Michael went on to tell how the two warriors had taken them to their village across the Ohio River. He talked about running the gauntlet and of Red

Hawk and White Feather, about his adoption, and how Mary had saved Red Hawk from the mama bear.

The Mohans were glad to have Michael and Mary back in camp, and the Ryans soon settled into a daily routine as days turned to weeks and weeks turned into years.

Mary went from a gangly twelve-year-old to a young woman of seventeen in what seemed like overnight to her father. She continued to learn about what it took to survive in the wilderness. Hermit Eeds showed her things no one else in the valley could, and Mary sharpened the skills taught to her by the Shawnee. By late summer of 1770, Mary could outshoot any man in camp. By the time the leaves began to change, a man entered Mohan's Camp who would change Mary's life forever.

Chapter 19

CHARLES MCLAIN

October 1770

Charles McLain was the most magnificent man Mary Ryan had ever seen. He wasn't tall but was powerfully built, with muscular arms, broad shoulders, a small waist, and blue eyes that melted her heart the first time she looked into them. He arrived at Mohan's Camp alone but with a head full of dreams of owning land on this frontier. Mary was afraid he might take off with others to Kentucky, but it was clear that Charles had other ideas after meeting her.

Mary was repairing her father's moccasins when Charles strolled into camp. She knew of his arrival before he entered camp, as her friend, the red hawk, kept an eye on her and let her know when strangers approached. She had the gift of being able to communicate with animals, and after she and her father left their adopted family, Red Hawk and White Feather, a red-tailed hawk appeared on the trail back to Mohan's Camp and followed them there. Mary knew that her uncle, the Shawnee chief Red Hawk, had something to do with it, and she liked having the bird around.

The others in camp eventually accepted her animal friends and left them alone. It was only difficult for her when new people came and she tried to explain it to them. Some believed her; others did not. She didn't want anything to happen to her animal friends, but it was difficult to keep the hunters from killing some of them, especially the large buck that hung around camp, who had a large rack of horns, at least twelve points. But he quickly learned to elude the hunters and their flintlocks.

The hawk circled McLain as he approached Mohan's Camp at the mouth of Mohan's Run. He heard the hawk's cry above him. What he wasn't ready for was the beautiful red-haired young woman at the edge of the trees, clad only in a man's shirt, breech-cloth, and leggings. When he heard the distinctive "click" of her flintlock as she pulled the hammer back and aimed it at his chest, he stopped dead in his tracks, his mouth open, more because of her beauty than the gun aimed at him.

"Stop right there, sir!" Mary had to be careful, as she was alone in camp. The others were out hunting the valley to the north. She wasn't afraid, just cautious. She knew the hawk was watching out for her and, sure enough, the hawk landed in a nearby tree, obviously watching the proceedings.

"My name is Charles McLain. I'm looking for the Mohan brothers," Charles said.

Mary knew he was telling the truth; she had a way of sizing people up quickly. "I'm sorry," she said. "One can't be too careful these days with what's going on." She gently let the hammer back to its resting place and lowered her weapon. "John didn't mention he was expecting anyone."

"He doesn't know about me, but I have heard about the Mohans and this place from friends," Charles offered.

"I suppose you must be hungry, Mr. McLain. Can I fix you a plate of stew?"

"Yes, I'd appreciate that. And please, call me Charles."

Charles could not take his eyes off Mary. Her auburn hair and her obvious female attributes were not well hidden under her clothing as she gathered her things in her bag. As he got closer to her, he became aware of her emerald-green eyes that seemed to smile back at him. She still had a lilting Irish brogue, and as she talked, he thought of his home, Scotland, and those he had left behind to come to this place. This place reminded him of the Scottish Highlands. In the large cities to the east, there were more people and a busier way of life, but this place had a mysterious feeling to it, like there were secrets hidden under every rock, behind each tree. There was much to learn in this new land, and McLain was up for anything.

Mary put her bag down and turned her attention to the large pot of stew in the center of camp that had been simmering since morning. The men would be home before long and looking for something to eat after their long hunt. Mary had Charles sit near the fire as she dished out a bowl of hot rabbit stew for him. She felt awkward in his presence, not knowing what to say. It was funny, here she was, a grown woman with various skills, acting like a schoolgirl with her first crush.

Mary had not had any suitors in this wild country, although there were men who had expressed an interest to her father. But Michael told them all no, telling all of them that his daughter would be the one to decide whom she married. Michael was protective of his daughter, even when he didn't have to be; she could hunt, shoot and ride as well or better than any of the men in camp and had proven it over and over. She had learned tracking and fighting skills from Old Man Eeds and the Shawnee. The men in camp respected her and her abilities and knew not to provoke her in any way. It was funny, though, when newcomers arrived and tried to put her "in her place." Most men thought women were beneath them, more of a possession than an equal. Mary was more than any man's equal; she could do things many of them could not.

Mary hoped Charles was not like the others. As she sat silently by the fire, watching Charles eat, she thought of what had happened in the past. More than once she'd had to wrestle a man who got out of line. One of the Mohans—or others in the camp—always goaded any man who showed an interest in her into challenging her to a contest of skills, knowing that the man would lose. Mary enjoyed competition and liked challenges but hated it when they did that to her.

Once, a large Frenchman had been in camp for two weeks, trying to get her alone. The hair on Mary's neck stood up every time she was in his presence. James Mohan told the Frenchman that the way to Mary's heart was through the competition that men enjoyed at Rendezvous, where they would appear to sell their furs and restock on items needed for their life on the frontier. These get-togethers included games of skill, shooting, knife and tomahawk throwing, races, and other contests. Mary reluctantly agreed to a shooting contest. After she won, the Frenchman became angry and came at her with his knife. Before the Mohans or her father could inter-cede, Mary managed to trip him as he came at her. She pulled her knife from its sheath and stood over him, her teeth clenched, her eyes blazing in anger. "We are through, Monsieur. I have nothing to prove to you!" With that, she had turned to James Mohan and said, "Never do that to me again!"

Pulling her thoughts back to the present, she thought about her friend, the large buck. She had heard only one shot this morning and prayed that her friend was safe. She always talked to him on the morning of the hunts and watched as the hunters left camp. She would say aloud, "Stay to the south," or "Stay to the west" as she walked about the camp. Somehow, the buck understood her and had managed to stay alive in the woods for all the years she had been in the camp.

He had been a small fawn when one of the hunters killed his mother, and he had been found in the woods by Mary and her father. He was almost dead when they found him, but Mary insisted on taking him back to camp and took over the duties of raising him. It broke her heart to see him trusting men yet knowing she had to let him leave camp when he was stronger. The next fall she told him it was time that he left to find a family of his own. She had to chase him out of camp, yelling at him to leave. She cried as she threw stones at him and saw that he was confused by the strange treatment he was receiving from this woman he loved. Finally, he snorted, stomped the ground, and fled into the woods. He would stroll into camp occasionally to visit but was always a little wary of the others in camp. Mary spent time with him at the creek, telling him what was going on, stroking his beautiful hide as she watched him grow year after year into the most magnificent buck in the entire Augusta County of Virginia.

The hunting party, including Mary's father, returned and came straight to the center of camp and the stew waiting for them. Mary introduced Charles to the Mohan brothers, who welcomed the strong young man eager to learn the ways of the frontier. John

Mohan showed Charles to one of the cabins, where Charles stowed his belongings and quickly returned to the fire. On the way he noticed a flower, purple in color, growing at the edge of the path. He picked it and put it in his bag. He waited as long as he could, until only Michael and John Mohan remained at the fire, before he presented it to Mary. He knew enough to first ask Michael if he might gift the flower to his daughter to thank her for his much needed and appreciated meal. Michael smiled and just nodded his head yes.

Charles had a Scottish brogue, and between his blue eyes and the way he talked, Mary was smitten with him already. He pulled the flower from his bag and handed it to her, saying, "Thank ye, lass, for the delicious meal! This flower reminds me of the Scottish Highlands and the purple thistle that grows there. Until today, nothing I have ever seen has surpassed the beauty of the thistle or the Highlands—until I saw you."

Mary started to blush and was thankful it was dark. She still blushed easily, and it got worse when someone noticed and mentioned it. "Thank you, Charles," she replied softly. She didn't know what else to say.

It would be the first of many purple flowers Charles McLain would gift to Mary.

Chapter 20

SIMON (BUTLER) KENTON

Summer of 1771

Simon Butler, as he was known now, sat by the fire at Mohan's Camp at the mouth of Mohan's Run in western Virginia. Also around the fire were the Mohan brothers, Richard Falls, Michael Ryan, Mary, and Charles McLain, who had arrived in camp the previous fall. Simon had not met the Scotsman during his earlier visit to Mohan's Camp.

Simon had met the Mohan brothers previously, and they had invited him to spend time with them at their camp before setting out for "Kain-tuck-ee," as they pronounced the land to the south of them. Simon introduced himself to the Mohans as Simon Butler, his alias since he had fled into the wilderness from eastern Virginia after believing he killed a man named William Leachman in a jealous rage over Ellen Cummins, whom they both loved. What a stroke of luck for Simon to find out that Michael Ryan's deceased wife, Mary, had been a Butler. Both Simon's father and Michael had come from the same area of Ireland, so Simon had firsthand knowledge to throw in to make it all sound real. Simon used that false connection to try to get closer to young Mary. He played himself to be a long-lost cousin, not too close for romance but close enough for her to feel comfortable with him. So far it had not worked.

Simon was trying to be polite to Charles, the newest resident of camp, but he couldn't keep his eyes off the red-haired young woman who sat next to him. He had wanted her since the first day he saw her two months before when he had visited the Mohans, but he knew she was not the type of woman to use and then discard. She was special. Her father had raised her since the death of her mother, and although she had spent most of her years in this wild country, and some of it with the Shawnee, she was still pure and untouched. He knew her father would kill any man who laid a hand on her unless the two were married; he knew that Mary would not allow that to happen unless she was in love and married. He was leaving and it was better that he kept his feelings for her to himself. Mostly, though, he stayed quiet because he had a deep dark secret, one he wasn't ready to share with Mary or anyone else, and he knew she would not want to be a part of it. Still, he already felt a jealous twinge when he saw the way Mary looked at Charles. He knew sparks were flying between them, and although he was leaving in the morning, a part of him wanted to stay to win her affections.

Charles was not as tall as Simon, but he a well-built, powerful man. He had come to this country in search of land. He had arrived a year ago from his native Scotland and still had a thick Scottish brogue.

Mary's eyes lit up when she looked at him; even her father noticed. Michael wasn't ready to let go of his daughter, but he knew he was getting up in years, and Mary was eighteen and still not married. The protective father in him didn't want to think of Mary with this man—or any other—but he knew she would eventually leave him and get married. But he didn't look forward to that day. It had been just the two of them for so many years now that it was difficult for him to think of sharing her with another.

Michael had also noticed Butler's interest in his daughter, but even though Simon Butler was somewhat of a celebrity, much like Daniel Boone, for some reason Mary didn't seem to notice his awkward attempts for her attention.

As the group around the campfire dwindled down one by one, Simon noticed Mary seemed distracted. She was paying less attention to McLain and had begun to pay more attention to him all of a sudden. There was urgency in her look and voice. It was as if she wanted to tell him something.

As the Mohans said goodnight and left for their cabin, Charles McLain, at the urging of Michael, announced that he was retiring for the night also. He didn't want to leave Mary alone with Simon, but he also didn't want to anger Michael, the man he hoped would be his father-in-law. Charles took one last look at the fiery redhead and then disappeared into the darkness.

Michael looked at his daughter with a knowing glance and said goodnight. He stopped to shake Simon's hand and wish him well on his journey to Kentucky. He knew Mary needed to speak to Simon, and although in polite society an unmarried woman would not be left alone with a man, this was the frontier and Michael knew his daughter could take care of herself. She was different from any other woman he had known, and he knew her destiny was beyond his control.

Mary waited until her father had gone down the trail and up the hill to their cabin before she spoke her first words to Simon. She said she hated to see him go but knew he must. She asked him for a favor—to promise her that he would look after Daniel Boone upon reaching his destination.

Simon looked puzzled, but he had heard of the young woman's abilities, not only in her hunting, marksmanship, and athletic accomplishments, but her uncanny ability to communicate with animals and to foresee the future. He wasn't sure if he understood how she did it, but he had witnessed many unusual things in the short time he had known Mary, and he didn't want to hurt her feelings by scoffing at her request. But he could not resist the opportunity to tease her. "If I didn't know any better, I'd think you had a hankerin' for ol' Daniel."

"Don't be silly," she replied. "You and I both know he's married. I just need you to promise."

Simon's expression turned dark as he quietly agreed to watch over his friend. "What makes you think he needs my help? Daniel's a good fighter himself."

Mary replied, "I can't explain how I know these things. I just know them." She went on to explain that Simon and Daniel needed to be careful, especially outside a fort. "Indians will try to kill him, and you'll need to help him to safety. You're the only one who can do that."

"What should I do?"

"Throw him at them."

Simon was confused. "Throw what at them?"

"Daniel. Throw Daniel at them!"

Simon was quiet for a moment and, although he still did not understand what she meant, he replied, "I promise to watch over Daniel, and if the Indians attack, I'll throw Daniel at them."

Mary went quiet as the tears welled up in her eyes and a large lump formed in her throat. "Now you mock me. I am not a child! This is a serious situation, and you act like you don't care. You are the only one who can save him, and if you don't do as I have asked, he will die!"

Simon wanted more than anything to pick Mary up in his arms and kiss the tears away. He felt so badly that he had hurt her. He knew this might be the last time he saw her, and he did not want this to be the last memory she had of him. "I'm sorry, Mary. You're right, this is serious, and I promise to take care of Daniel. I won't let anything happen to him."

Mary was relieved. She took a long look into the eyes of the large man before her and knew he would do everything in his power to keep Daniel Boone safe. "Thank you, Simon."

Simon saw Mary's green eyes sparkle as she spoke to him. He leaned down to kiss her, and as he did, she closed her eyes as their lips met and wrapped her arms around his neck. Simon was lost in the moment, wishing it would never end. For a moment time stood still as their bodies melted into each other, but the howl of a nearby wolf broke the spell.

Mary let go of Simon, pushed him away from her, and said, "Thank you." She acted like nothing had happened. "Goodnight, Mr. Butler," she said primly and turned toward her cabin.

Mr. Butler? She hadn't called him that since the first day they met. Simon knew it was over before it had started. He would never have any more of Mary than he'd just had. She would marry Charles McLain, and Simon would never again taste her sweet lips or touch her magnificent body.

Mary turned as if remembering one last detail and said quietly, "Simon, you should be true to yourself and claim what is yours." At first he thought she meant that he should claim her as his woman. Then she took a step back in his direction as if she didn't want anyone else to hear what she had to say. "Simon, I know you're not a distant relative of mine or of any other Butlers. You have been living a lie, one that you must correct before you can be the man you're meant to be."

He knew now that she meant he should claim his real name—Kenton—rather than using the name Butler to hide his true identity.

Mary surprised Simon by what she said, but he was relieved at the same time. He hated to lie to anyone, especially Mary, but how could she know? He had not told anyone of the troubles he'd had before leaving home, of the fight where he killed his rival, the older man who married his true love. *She must be a witch*, he thought.

There was a lengthy period of silence before Mary spoke again. "I promise that your secret is safe with me, Simon, but it is not what you think it to be."

It is not what you think it to be. Simon rolled that sentence around his head three or four times as he watched Mary walk up the path to her cabin. *What does she mean?* Simon kept asking himself. It would be years before he knew the answer to that question. The wolf howled once more as Simon watched Mary walked toward her cabin. She stopped once and turned her head in the direction of the wolf's call. It was if they were having a conversation, and Simon knew that conversation did not include him. He called after her, "Goodnight, sweet Mary."

She turned toward him once again and said, "Goodnight, Simon."

The fire crackled as she once more turned and walked away. Simon closed his eyes, and thoughts of their kiss filled his head as he touched his hand to his lips. He would savor this moment for years to come. Mary Ryan was not ever going to be his, but he would never forget her or the time they spent together. She was one of a kind, and he hoped this would not be the last time they saw each other.

As she disappeared up the trail, the wolf let out one more howl, as if to say goodnight to Mary.

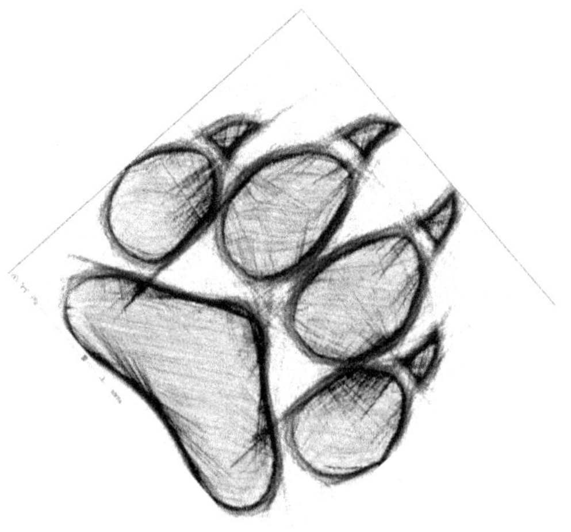

Chapter 21

THE HANDFASTING

July 17, 1771

Michael Ryan had mixed feelings about what his daughter was doing today. He loved her with all his heart, and he had known this day would eventually come, but he wasn't sure if he was ready to share his daughter with another man. He knew Mary loved Charles and Charles loved her, but that didn't make it any easier for him to give his daughter away today to the man who would be her husband.

Since there were no pastors living locally, the Mohans sent for Reverend John Sutton, who served as the preacher of a Baptist Church almost twenty miles southeast of the Mohan settlement. Although both Mary and Charles were Catholic, there were no priests in the area, so Reverend Sutton would have to suffice. Charles had proposed a handfasting during the ceremony, an ancient custom symbolizing unity that dated back to the ancient Celts. Mary loved the idea and had been working on the ribbons that would tie their hands together in the handfasting. She chose pieces of Charles' tartan cloth and strips of white cloth that had been a part of her mother's wedding dress.

The large field at the mouth of Mohan's Run was the site of the wedding. Reverend Sutton performed the ceremony to the point where the couple would exchange vows. Then Michael stepped forward to tie the ribbons around Mary's and Charles' hands. The couple exchanged vows, lovingly removed the ribbons, and returned them to Michael. The young couple could not afford wedding rings, and Mary cried when her father then offered his wedding ring to Charles and her mother's to her. To Mary, this made the ceremony perfect.

The celebration lasted into the evening, with the newlyweds, Michael, the Mohans, and the locals feasting, toasting, and enjoying a break from their difficult daily regimen. Even though the area had enjoyed mostly peaceful relations with the Indians since the end of Pontiac's War in 1765, there were still occasional raids, forcing the people of western Virginia to be ever cautious when they were hunting, cutting trees, farming, or doing what they needed to do to survive during these times.

Michael had offered to give the young couple his cabin on the hillside, and he and Charles had spent time together cutting logs and building a new, smaller cabin for Michael below the larger one. It gave them both time to get to know each other, and both were thankful for the chance to bond as father-in-law and son-in-law.

Although Charles enjoyed the wedding and was glad to see Mary so happy, he could not help but grow a little impatient as the celebration continued. He wanted to climb the hill to their cabin and finally take his wife into his arms and make love to her. He was also a little nervous. He knew Mary was a virgin and would not have any earlier lovers to compare him to, but he wanted this night to be special for her.

Finally! Charles could not believe that it was Michael himself who suggested that Charles take Mary home. He knew Michael was fond of him, but he also knew that, as a father, he had not relished the idea of a man lying with his daughter. After the couple thanked everyone and said their goodnights, Mary hugged and kissed her father. Then the newlyweds climbed the hill together as man and wife.

Charles opened the door to their cabin, picked up Mary, and carried her over the threshold. She giggled as he set her down, then they kissed passionately. Mary was nervous also. She wanted to please her husband but did not know what to expect. Without her mother, Mary did not have the benefit of an experienced woman to explain what happens between a man and a woman.

Charles lit a candle on the table, took off his shirt, then tried to get his wife out of her wedding dress. They both giggled as he fumbled with the small buttons on the back of the dress. Eventually, they both stood there naked, looking at each other, Charles taking in every small detail of his wife's body. Her breasts were white and her pink nipples were erect. Her body was small but muscular. He reached up to loosen the ribbons in her hair to let her magnificent red hair fall around her shoulders. Then he picked her up again and placed her in their bed, and as he did, Mary began kissing him. The two young lovers began exploring each other's bodies.

First, Charles touched her breasts, then kissed them. Mary rolled onto her back and Charles moved on top of her as she spread her legs, inviting her husband to take the one gift she could only give once—her virginity. Charles entered her slowly, trying not to hurt her. Mary was not prepared for the pain at first, but she also did not expect the pleasure she quickly felt.

They made love three times that night. Mary woke the next morning to her husband kissing her neck, and she smiled, knowing this man loved her. He seemed eager to resume their lovemaking, but as much as Mary hated to tell her husband no, she explained that she was a little sore from their shared passions of the previous night and thought it wise to wait a bit. She kissed him, got up and dressed quickly, and began making her husband breakfast for the first time.

After their first night together, their routine was the same every day. Charles would rise before daybreak, light the candle, a fire if necessary, and Mary would make breakfast. Charles would either go hunting with his father-in-law or check with the Mohan brothers to see what they needed him to do for the camp. In the mornings after Charles left, a large, silver-gray female wolf would come out of the woods and sit, looking toward the cabin.

Mary had noticed the wolf one morning when she went outside to gather firewood. She had seen the wolf in the area the last few months but never this close, and she was surprised to see her and amazed that the wolf didn't run away. She began talking to the wolf, at first staying on the porch as she greeted her new friend. Every day the conversation grew longer and, gradually, Mary got closer to the she-wolf until one day she was close enough to lean down to touch her. It was as if they had been friends for years. Mary could pet the wolf and rub her belly, and the wolf would nudge her with her nose.

It wasn't long before Mary started telling the wolf to be careful, to stay away when the men were near. Mary never saw the larger male gray wolf who waited for his mate nearby in the woods, but at night Mary would hear them calling to each other, and she finally had to tell Charles about the wolves and plead with him not to hurt them.

Mary sewed shirts for her husband and began wearing his older ones. One day Charles came home earlier than usual and caught Mary making a small garment. He stopped in his tracks, a smile lighting up his face. "Do you have something to tell me?"

Mary stopped what she was doing, placed the material on the table, stood up, put her arms around her husband, and smiled. "You're going to be a father."

They kissed passionately, then Charles picked up his wife and carried her to their bed. But before they got past the kissing, he stopped, looked at the beautiful face of his wife, and his smile faded. "Will we hurt the wee one?"

"No," replied Mary, smiling.

Charles and Mary lost themselves again in each other's love, as they would frequently until Mary became so large that just getting around the cabin became difficult for her.

As the spring of 1772 turned into the fall of 1772, Charles and Mary enjoyed each day together as they looked forward to their child's birth in the winter. Mary continued to make clothes for the baby, whom she knew she would name Ryan. She knew she was having a boy. Even when others said she was carrying a girl, Mary knew better. She could not wait until he was born so that she and Charles could hold and love him. Her father had made them a cradle for the baby, and everything was in place as they waited for the day their son would be born.

Chapter 22

DIGGING TURTLE

January 1773

Digging Turtle sat by the campfire, one thought on his mind: he was going to kill every Ryan he could find. He would get even with the men who had killed his father, uncle, and brother. Michael Ryan, his daughter, and Michael's brother, John, would pay for the deaths of Snapping Turtle, his uncle Running Badger, and his older brother, Red Turtle.

Red Turtle had been living in Red Wing's village since he married, and he was alone on the trail outside the village when he was surprised by the Indian killer, John Ryan, who cut his throat and left him for dead. Fortunately for Digging Turtle, he came upon his brother before he died. The wound on his neck did not totally sever either artery, and Red Turtle was able to tell him who his attacker was—John Crow Ryan. Michael and John Ryan were now responsible for killing three members of Digging Turtle's family and Digging Turtle vowed he would make these whites pay for what they had done.

John Ryan was a well-known Indian killer, like Lewis Wetzel. Both men made it their lifelong duty to kill Indians in retaliation for the killing of their family members by Indians. Now it was Digging Turtle's turn to even the score. He had only been a boy when his chief, Red Hawk, adopted Michael Ryan as his brother. That didn't sit well with Digging Turtle and his father, Snapping Turtle, since Michael had killed Snapping Turtle's brother, Running Badger, when captured. While living with the Shawnee, Michael Ryan and Snapping Turtle had been at odds with each other over Running Badger's death. They eventually fought and Snapping Turtle died as a result. Not long after that, Michael and his daughter returned to the white world. Michael had lived near the Mohan brothers' camp before the Shawnee took him and his daughter captive, which is where John Ryan found them. Digging Turtle would go to the Mohans' camp, kill Michael Ryan, his daughter, his brother, and anyone else he could find.

It was the middle of winter and the trip would be difficult, but it would be worth it to cut the throats of the brothers who had taken so much from him. He knew that Michael Ryan had remained on friendly terms with the Shawnee and his adopted brother, Red Hawk. He also knew that Michael's daughter, the one with the long, flowing red hair, was a woman now and probably had a family of her own. Digging Turtle would go where they lived and exact his revenge on the Ryans for what they had done. He thought it better to go alone; he would be able to travel more quickly by himself.

Digging Turtle prepared for his trek east. He had his knife, tomahawk, dried meat, water, and the medicine pouch he wore around his neck. He knew he would not get permission from Red Hawk, but he didn't need it or want it. He would slip out of the village before daybreak. It wasn't unusual for warriors to go raiding the white settlers, as so much had been taken from them. The British had talked his leaders into siding with them against the French, but the British had never kept their promises. The whites continued to pour into the land that once was their hunting grounds. They took whatever they wanted, destroyed the forests, and killed the game.

Digging Turtle was going to revenge the deaths of his family and enjoy shedding Ryan blood.

Chapter 23

THE HUNT

January 15, 1773

Mary had not slept well the past couple of nights. It was to be expected, as she was full with child and everything had become an effort for the young woman. She remembered her dreams most nights and the previous night's was no exception. She shuddered when the images ran through her mind just as the sun was trying to peek into the window of the cabin where she and Charles slept. She saw her beloved husband on a nearby hill, taking aim at the large buck close to him. In her dream she heard the shot, saw the deer fall, and then saw only the deep scarlet color of blood. But it was not the blood of the deer; it was Charles' blood. She sat straight up in bed as she realized what she had seen, and the scream that burst from her lips woke Charles. As she looked into his blue eyes, she saw a flash of bright light then the face of a warrior, one she had seen before. She felt a deep stabbing pain in her right side and then heard footsteps.

Charles had learned to take his wife seriously when she "saw" things then tried to explain them to him. He could tell she had had another one of her dreams, and he waited for her to explain what had happened. This time Mary was silent, but the fear in her eyes told him everything he needed to know. He had plans to hunt today with his father-in-law. Mary had been asking him not to go for the last three days, and he expected more of the same this morning.

"Mary, I know what you're going to say, but I need to go today with your father. We're out of meat, and I don't want to be gone and miss the birth of our son, so today is the best day for our hunt."

To the best of their knowledge, Mary was not due for another week or two, but she had been experiencing the normal nesting habits of late-term pregnant women. She had also been having some kind of nightmare the past few nights, but she refused to share them with her husband. "Please, Charles, don't go today!"

The look in Mary's eyes frightened Charles since he knew his wife was not afraid of anything or anyone. He blamed it on the pregnancy, but deep down he felt an impending doom in his own heart. However, it was one he would not admit to, especially to Mary. "I must go today. Besides, your father has been looking forward to getting out in the hills again after being cooped up the last few months."

Michael had not been feeling well, and Mary was concerned about his health. She had tried to doctor him, but he was too busy these days, trying to get everything in order for his first grandchild. He was living in the smaller cabin that he and Charles had built a little farther down the hill from the larger cabin he had given the newlyweds. Mary was glad he was close by and felt guilty that he had given up his home for them, but her father had insisted. He had also made a cradle for the baby, just like the one he had made for Mary when she was born. It was beautiful and Mary could hardly wait to see her son lying in it beside the bed of his parents.

"We'll only hunt this morning, I promise. We'll be back in time for lunch."

Mary wanted to tell Charles what she had seen, but she was afraid that if she spoke the words aloud, the terrible images she had seen would become reality. Right now they were just a part of her nightmares. "Please promise me that you'll be careful." Mary pleaded with her husband both with her words and with her eyes. She loved him with all her heart and had thanked the Creator just last night for the blessings He had bestowed upon her, her father, her husband, and soon, a son.

Charles promised that he would be careful as he dressed, and while he gathered his accoutrements, Mary got out of bed and made him breakfast. Charles scolded her for her efforts but was secretly glad that she still doted on him. Although both husband and wife didn't mention the hunt again, both seemed on edge. Mary wanted to get on her knees and beg Charles not to go, but she knew him well enough to know it would not do any good. Charles would rather stay home in their warm cabin with his wife but had promised his father-in-law that they would hunt together today and did not want to disappoint him. Charles and Michael had become friends in addition to being related by marriage. The young man looked up to Michael and respected him. Michael was Charles' surrogate father in this new land, and Charles was thankful for their relationship. Michael was also thankful to have Charles in his life and for the comfort he had knowing that the young man genuinely loved his daughter and would take care of her.

As Charles finished his breakfast, Mary tried to hide her feelings from him. As they stood before the door, both spoke at the same time. Mary asked Charles to go first. "Take care of yourself while I am gone. Go back to bed and stay warm. There are no chores that must be done until I get back, and I'll do them then. Don't worry, everything will be fine. Your father and I will bring home meat for the table so that you can stay strong and healthy to feed our son."

Both Charles and Mary pictured her holding a suckling baby to her breast as they enjoyed the warmth of their cabin. "I'm sorry to be such a worry," Mary said softly. "I suppose it has more to do with my pregnancy than anything else, but I still wish you—"

Charles put his fingers to her lips before she finished her sentence. He had learned things from his young wife since they met over two years ago, and he had heard her predict things that had come true. If she didn't say what he knew she was thinking, maybe it wouldn't come true. He took his hand from her mouth and pressed his lips to hers with an urgency Mary had not felt in these past few months. They both held their embrace longer than usual, eyes closed, hearts open. Mary would remember this kiss the rest of her life. In the future, she would curse herself for not making Charles stay home. Now she silently cursed him for going, and she cursed her father for wanting to go. Finally, the kiss ended, their eyes locked, and they both said "I love you" at the same time.

Although it was cold this January morning, Mary stood at the open door to watch her husband leave. Charles turned around to get one last glimpse of his wife and started to scold her for being out in the cold but instead decided to call back to her, "I love you, my darling, and our son. I'll be home soon." He smiled at her, his blue eyes taking in her beauty as he descended the hill to the next cabin.

Mary didn't want to close the cabin door. She knew that when she did, it would close this chapter of her life. A pain began in her chest as the door closed. She tried to ignore it, but it took her breath away. She wondered if it was too late to catch her husband. Surely, he would stay home now. She took a step toward the door, and as she did, a wave of nausea swept across her. The room began to spin, and she felt like she was going to faint. Mary managed to get to the bed, where she collapsed. She tried to call out to Charles, but with the door closed and the wind blowing, he could not hear her pleas. She closed her eyes shut and fell into a deep sleep.

Farther down the hill, Charles and Michael stepped out of the new cabin. Charles had thought he had heard something and asked Michael if he had heard it. Both listened intently but there was no sound except the wind blowing. Both men knew if they climbed the hill to the cabin where Mary was waiting for them, they would not be able to ignore her requests not to go. It was a decision both would live to regret before the sun had fully risen.

Chapter 24

THREE DEATHS

January 15, 1773

Michael Ryan and Charles McLain walked the short distance from Michael's cabin down the hill and across the open field that had been the site of the wedding and once had been the site of a "Rendezvous" between the white men and the Indians. They crossed the small stream now called Mohan's Run and started up the steep hill west of the cabins. Game was still plentiful in these beautiful hills in this part of western Virginia. The air was crisp and cold, a new snow had fallen during the night, and, as they walked, the clouds lifted to let the stars shine through. This was Charles' favorite time of day, just before the sun came up. Both men walked in silence, more because of what was on their minds than to not scare the game. It was five minutes before either man spoke.

Charles spoke first. "Mary seemed more restless last night and this morning than usual. Is that normal for women who are close to term?"

The older man's brow furrowed as he tried to remember his wife, Mary, in her last days of pregnancy. "I suppose most women get a little more sensitive when their time comes, but your Mary is different from most women," Michael said.

That fact was at once clear to Charles the first time he saw Mary, and it was proven to him daily. He knew his wife had a gift, multiple gifts in fact, which allowed her to do things other people could not. She had also spent years with the Shawnee, learning their ways, and she knew things before they happened. It put most people on edge around her until they got to know her better. They did not trust her. People called her a witch. Michael and Charles both knew she was not a witch; she was a good, kind-hearted woman who gave more of herself to others in a week than most did in a lifetime. She did have strange abilities, but both men had grown to accept them—and usually listened to her when she pushed—but this time they had ignored her, blaming her fears on her pregnancy.

The light began to peek over the trees to the east as the men reached the top of the large hill. There were deer signs present on the worn path. The hunters had a choice of settling in somewhere close to the path to wait for the deer to come back on their way to their bedding areas or following the tracks in hopes of catching sight of a large buck. They quietly discussed their plans and decided one should stay here and the other one should follow the largest set of prints. Charles offered to go after the buck and let Michael stay put since he still did not feel well. Michael was grateful to the younger man, and knew why he had made that choice, but he felt like his worth to the family was diminishing as his health deteriorated. The men hugged each other as they often did, wished each other well, and agreed to meet back at this spot in two hours' time unless one heard the other's shot, at which time they would rendezvous where the deer was.

Michael settled in near the path at the edge of the woods, trying to stay warm as his son-in-law followed the path along the ridgeline. Both men's thoughts were on Mary. Michael spent the first few minutes daydreaming about his first grandchild. He pictured a handsome boy learning the ways of the frontiersmen, with his mother's red hair and with her special abilities. He drifted off to sleep as Charles followed the deer tracks.

Charles thought of Mary with each step. He was cautious not to make a sound, but his mind was back at the cabin. Suddenly, he spotted the large buck, his head down as he grazed a little more on the grass before bedding down for the day. With his head down, the buck did not see the approaching hunter, and the wind was behind the buck, blowing in Charles' direction, and Charles was stepping quietly across the forest floor. The buck could not see, hear, or smell the man about to kill him. It was the perfect shot.

The large deer lifted his head for an instant just as Charles brought his muzzle-loader to his shoulder. He saw his wife in his mind's eye, standing at the door of their cabin just as he had left her less than an hour ago. As he closed his left eye to shoot, he heard his wife's voice as plain as if she were standing there next to him. "Charles!" It was more of a shout. His finger squeezed the trigger, he heard the shot fire, and smoke bellowed from the end of his gun as he held it steady after the shot. The buck dropped to the ground at the same time that Charles felt a sharp pain in his right side. He had been so intent on shooting the buck, and so distracted by thoughts of Mary, that he did not hear the Shawnee sneak up on him.

The Indian tried to thrust his knife into the white man again, this time in his chest, hoping for a lethal blow, but Charles was strong and "had a fire in his belly" when it came to fighting, and he managed to block the strike. Both men struggled for their lives as the Indian tried to plunge his knife into the white man again. Charles's gun had fallen to his side in the struggle but was no good to him unloaded unless he could get to it and strike his adversary with the butt end. He also had a knife, which he drew from its sheath and struck out at the man trying to kill him. Charles had lost a large amount of blood already and was losing his strength as each second ticked by. He did not give up, as he knew that his family depended on him, and thoughts of his wife, child, and father-in-law kept pushing into his brain. A planned blow to the Indian's chest was thwarted, but the knife still cut the red man's flesh as Charles fought for his life. A large cut on the left side of the Shawnee's face began to spill out so much blood that he could not see from his left eye. Both men struggled, spilling their blood on the other. Charles could feel his life ebbing from him as he reached for the man's throat. He grabbed the muscled throat, trying to choke the Indian, but his strength was leaving his body, just as his spirit was.

Charles pulled at the leather thong around the man's neck as the Indian turned his head in the direction of sounds he heard coming toward him. Someone was coming through the woods at a quick pace. The Shawnee needed to leave. He was in no shape to fight off another man. One more thrust of his knife was all he had time for, and the cold metal weapon found its target in the back of Charles McLain.

Charles fell to the ground, the knife still in his back. The Indian wanted to scalp his foe but realized he didn't have time for that before the approaching man reached the clearing carpeted with red blood. In the last seconds of their struggle, he did not notice that his medicine pouch was gone from his neck. He didn't even dare stop to pick up his knife. He needed to make a quick escape through the woods.

Michael was awakened from his sleep by the unmistakable sound of a shot. He opened his eyes, startled at first as he came out of his dream, but soon realized he was at the edge of the woods at the top of the hill in the bitter cold January morning and not in the warmth of his cabin, gazing into the blue eyes of his grandson. The sound of the shot came from some distance away to the north, and it would take the old man some time to reach his son-in-law. He got up as quickly as his old joints would let him and started making his way up the path to where he knew fresh meat for their camp would be waiting for him.

The familiar pain in his chest started as he climbed a small incline on the ridge, but he hurried on. The quicker he reached Charles, the quicker the two men could return home with their meat, and the quicker they could dispel the fears of his daughter. As Michael grew closer to where he calculated Charles was, he heard another movement farther ahead. It must be Charles getting the carcass ready to carry off the hill. Charles had quickly learned the ways of the frontier and had grown adept at supplying meat, dressing it in the field and getting it home to his family.

Before Michael rounded the path to the small clearing where just five minutes ago Charles had lost his struggle with the Indian, Michael had an impending feeling of doom. As he entered the clearing, the sight before him seemed surreal. Charles was lying on the ground, blood everywhere. The deer was by the edge of the woods to the north of his son-in-law, also lying in its own blood. Michael quickened his step to a full run until he reached Charles. The young man was still alive, but Michael knew that if he didn't get aid soon, he would die. The knife was still protruding from the young man's muscled back. Michael quickly pulled the knife from Charles' back, and his first impulse was to toss it as far as he could, but his instincts told him to keep it, so he slid it into his belt. He didn't realize there were two wounds until he picked up Charles and saw blood on his hunting shirt where he had been stabbed the first time.

The older man found the source of bleeding and tried to put pressure on the wound, but there were two openings spilling the younger man's blood, one on his right side and one on his back near the spine. Michael picked up Charles, saying, "Don't worry, lad, I'll get you home." He figured he could put Charles over his shoulder, put pressure on the first wound with his own body, and try to put pressure on the second wound with his left hand as he carried his son-in-law down the hill.

The adrenaline was flowing as Michael made his way down the path toward home. He was practically running by the time he hit the flat ground of the open field. He saw John Mohan heading in his direction as he made his way across the field, but there wasn't enough wind left in his lungs to yell to John that he needed help. He wondered why Mohan was heading for him to begin with. Michael thought maybe Mary had gone into labor, and John had been sent to fetch the hunters. All this effort took its toll on Michael as he struggled to stay on his feet. The pain exploded in his chest as he reached his friend. John Mohan had seen many frightening things in these hills, but judging from the look on his face, he had never seen anything like this.

Michael Ryan had stopped running, his face ashen in color, blood covering both him and his burden. He gently laid Charles on the ground and began to put pressure on the wounds. He could barely speak as the pain grew in intensity. He held Charles in his arms as his son-in-law's life poured from his body.

As his life was ebbing, in his mind Charles saw Mary writhing in pain in their cabin, the baby unable to release itself from his mother's body. The cord was wrapped around his neck. Mary had been alone when the pains started. Anthony Mohan had made a habit of checking on her frequently during the day and had knocked on her door almost a half hour after labor pains took over her body. There were no other women in camp at this time, meaning Anthony and Mary would have to deal with this alone.

John fired off his pistol as a signal to the others in camp to give a hand. Richard Falls and a couple of other men ran toward the three figures. As they reached them, Michael looked up, tears in his eyes, pleading for help. "Dear Heavenly Father, help us!"

Richard assessed the situation, picked up Charles, and told John Mohan and Luke Scott to help Michael the rest of the way to home. Unknown to all four of them in the field, Mary was fighting a battle of her own to save her son.

Michael reached the door of Mohan's cabin as John was taking Charles' hunting shirt off. There was blood everywhere. Michael could hardly breathe, and Luke pulled out a chair for the older man to sit on. The elder Mohan started to bandage the bleeding wounds as Charles opened his eyes to speak. "Mary, Mary!"

Meanwhile, Anthony Mohan was struggling to turn the baby inside Mary. The pain was more than she had ever experienced. She shut her eyes, letting her mind drift from the pain, and as she did, she saw the face of her beloved husband, Charles, and heard his cry for her. "Charles!" she called. She also saw the faces of her parents, Michael and Mary, and she called to them.

Michael Ryan closed his eyes and thoughts of his sweet daughter, her mother, Mary, and Ireland came flooding into his mind, then the face of a baby came to him, and he knew it was his grandson, Ryan. He could faintly hear what was going on in John Mohan's cabin, but he didn't want to open his eyes. He wanted to stay where he was. He now saw his wife walking softly across the green field near the Rock of Cashel, calling "Michael Ryan," as she had done a hundred times before. The light around her grew in intensity, the feelings of warmth and love surrounded him. The pull of his wife was too strong for Michael, and he succumbed to it. As he reached out to touch his wife, he noticed for the first time that Charles, his son-in-law, was beside her, carrying a baby with red hair.

John Mohan worked with speed and purpose to close the gaping wounds in Charles. At first they didn't even notice that Michael's head had fallen forward on his chest, but when they did, they thought he must be in prayer. It wasn't until Charles took his last gasp of air, said his wife's name, "Mary," then closed his eyes did they notice their old friend had stopped breathing too.

Mary let out a low growl as she pushed one last time to free herself of the body of her beloved son. As she did, a white light overcame her, the pain was gone, and she felt cool wind blow past her ears. She heard the haunting melody of a fiddle playing in the background and felt hands touching her gently. She thought she surely must be dying. She was in the cool green field below the Rock of Cashel, where she had played as a child. Her father, Michael, and her mother, Mary, were walking towards her, smiling as they got closer. Behind them she saw her Charles, and he was carrying something—a baby with red hair. *NO!* She felt her mind screaming, not sure if her lips had made the sound too. This meant she was dead, as were her father, husband, and son. This must be a nightmare. She would wake from this one, too, as she had from all the others. But as she gazed into the faces of her loved ones, she knew this was not one of her normal dreams.

Her mother spoke to her. "Lass, it is not your time yet." Mary wanted to reach out to them, especially Charles and the baby, but as she did, the pain returned. She felt an enormous pressure in her body and a pulling sensation she could not ignore. Slowly, she began to hear the actual sounds of her cabin, the fire crackling, and not the beautiful fiddle tune she had been hearing. The bright light faded as did the faces of her family. She cried out—but in vain.

Anthony Mohan had his hands full, and despite all his efforts, the red-haired baby boy was lying motionless in a small blanket in his mother's arms. The blood-curdling cry from the young woman's lips sent chills down Mohan's spine. He had no way of knowing that, at that very instant, the Creator chose to take Mary's family in entirety in one quick swoop of the death angel.

Chapter 25

THE FUNERALS

January 18, 1773

The entire Mohan's Camp was in a state of shock, as was the surrounding area all the way to Prickett's Settlement. The deaths of Mary's husband, father, and son were more than anyone could bear to think about, but it had to be done. The Mohan brothers and family did their best to console Mary, but it was more than they were equipped for. It took them a while to sort out what they knew about what happened and what they surmised. After talking to Mary, and hearing her version of her nightmares, they were convinced that Charles' attacker was Shawnee. Michael had succumbed to a heart ailment, and the baby died in childbirth, as often happened on this frontier.

Mary knew better. They were right about one thing, though, it was a Shawnee who had murdered her husband, but he had also murdered her father and baby. Michael would not have died if he had not carried her husband so far, and the baby would have lived if not for the nightmares Mary had been having. It was a curse come true, and Mary knew who would pay.

James Mohan had found a knife in Michael's belt which they figured must have been the one that killed Charles. Michael must have pulled it out before bringing his son-in-law down from the mountain. They also found a small leather bag in Charles' hand and debated whether or not to give it to Mary. They knew they should, but they wanted to wait until after the funerals later that day.

Mary changed that plan. As they prepared to leave for the funerals, Mary asked James and John Mohan if they were forgetting something. They both looked at her then at each other. She knew! "I want what you have found on my father and husband."

How did she know? She wasn't guessing; she asked for the knife and medicine bag. They pleaded with her to wait, but she would not take no for an answer. They had cleaned the blood off the knife and had wrapped both objects in a cloth. Their first thought was to bury them with Charles and Michael, but now they would have to give them to Mary. There would be no peace until they did.

The Mohans asked Mary to wait until after the funerals to look at them, and she gave in on this one request. She wanted to be alone when she opened the cloth and touch the objects that had been a part of taking three lives. She put them away in a trunk in her cabin before following the men up the mountain.

The few women who braved the trip to Mohan's Camp were insisting that Mary stay behind. She was still bleeding from the childbirth, the weather was cold, she was weak. Their stupid chattering was driving her insane. They already thought she was insane, she had heard them say so, but she knew better. There was no one left on this earth who could sway her mind now. She had been fiercely independent before and would be more so now. No one could tell her what to do, not these women, not the Mohans, not even Old Man Eeds if he were here. *No one!* She was going to the top of the hill to the funerals and that was final.

The land was cold and hard from the winter chill, but they had managed to dig two graves at the top of the hill east of camp. Mary had asked that the baby be buried with his father. She saw to it that her father was buried in his suit he had worn for their wedding, Charles in his kilt, and Ryan in one of the outfits she had made for him. The cemetery was in a perfect spot overlooking the entire valley.

The mountain was too steep for a cart to make it up the side and riding a horse up the damp and slippery grass was not an option, but Mary insisted on going to the top to lay her family to rest. The men carried the wooden caskets with their precious cargo, and Mary walked behind. The frosty winter wind blew her red hair, even from under her hooded cape, but Mary did not care. It made her numb, and she was beginning to like that feeling.

"The poor woman—" Mary had heard it more than she could bear. People didn't mean to hurt her, but she heard them in their hushed tones talking about her as if she were dead too. She might as well be. Then a thought came to her, one she knew she shouldn't be having, but still, it penetrated her skull just like the knife had Charles' back. She would kill the man responsible for this if it was the last thing she ever did! It was the one thought in her mind that kept her going, kept her sanity in all this craziness surrounding her. All the way up to the graves, Mary plotted her escape from these people and the sweet revenge she would extract from killing the man responsible for putting her family in those graves.

James Mohan spoke comforting words over the graves of his friends, but the wind insisted on blowing his words off down the mountain and into the valley floor below. Part of Mary was listening—the part of her that was still rational—but that part was growing smaller as time wore on. She shed no tears on the mountain. Her tears were behind her now. She was a warrior and must prepare for battle. Even in her emotional state, she was thinking clearly. These people would hover over her and drive her crazier than she already was, but eventually, they would have to get on with their lives, as people always did, and leave the bereaved to their mourning. She would start gathering her things for the trip—her bundle, her weapons, food and water, *and* the knife and medicine pouch taken from the man she sought.

She closed her eyes as Mohan finished his prayer. She silently said her own prayer. "Father, forgive me for what I am about to do."

Chapter 26

THE INDIAN CAVE

February 1, 1773

An exhausted and senseless Mary Ryan McLain fell to the cave floor. She had walked from Mohan's Camp the three miles to the old Indian Cave where she used to play as a child. Old Man Eeds had shown it to her, and as far as she knew, no one else knew of its existence. It had been used by the ancient ones, the ones who lived here before the Shawnee and other tribes claimed this land as their hunting ground. They left marks or petroglyphs on the walls, carvings of human figures, animals, and animal tracks. She had been fascinated with these as a child, running her fingers along the indents on the rock, imagining the people who had placed them there. She was too exhausted to even look at them tonight.

She had crept out of camp in the dark of night with one thing on her mind: revenge for the deaths of her father, husband, and newborn son. She hadn't been in her right mind or she would never have undertaken such a trip in her weakened state. She was still weak from childbirth, and her emotional state would be described by the locals as "touched in the head." She carried only the bare necessities: a blanket, food, water, her medicine bundle, her flintlock, and a knife. Her friend, the red hawk, followed her from camp, as did the silver-gray she-wolf, both watching as she stumbled along the path by the water. The hawk cried out to her in vain. Mary had trouble making it up the steep embankment with all that she carried and barely managed to get into the small opening of the cave before she collapsed.

She slipped in and out of a fitful sleep, not sure what was real or what was a dream. She saw the face of Charles as he took aim at the big buck in front of him. As he pulled the trigger, she heard him silently say a prayer to Grandfather to thank him for the blessings He had given him: this buck before him that would supply meat to the camp, his new wife, Mary, and their unborn child, and his life here on the western Virginia frontier. Mary watched as the rifle ball found its way to its target and then watched as a knife plunged into her husband's right side. She knew he hadn't felt the pain, only the pressure of the blade going in, and when he realized what was happening and turned to face his attacker, Mary saw the attacker's face too. It was a face she knew.

Mary continued to watch as the two men struggled. The buck fell where he had stood; a perfect shot had taken his life. She knew that, normally, Charles was more cautious in the woods. He should have heard the Indian creeping up on him, but his mind had been focused on her and their new baby that would soon be born. Charles had told her he was the happiest man in all of Virginia. He was married to the beautiful Mary Ryan, who was going to give him a son any day now, and he loved the life they had made together.

All of this, Mary saw in her dreams as she lay near death herself. *Death would be a welcome relief to the pain,* she thought. But as she thought of dying and being reunited with her mother, father, Charles, and the baby, she gained strength, strength she would need to see her plan through. When the Mohans had given her the medicine bag they found on Charles' body, Mary knew the man who killed her beloved husband was the Shawnee named Digging Turtle. Mary had never wanted anything more than the death of this man who had caused her so much pain. She could go to her adopted Shawnee uncle's village and demand justice for what had been done, and better yet, she would stalk the murderer like he had stalked her husband and kill him with his own knife.

She knew that hating was wrong. She had lived both sides of the white man versus Indian struggle on this frontier, and she had people on both sides she loved, but she had to kill Digging Turtle. She was certain that the blood that ran in her veins was the same blood that ran in her white uncle's, the one they called "Indian Killer Ryan."

Mary drifted off again, tormented by her thoughts. Sometime during the night, she heard a wolf howl, and later felt the warmth of something lying beside her.

Chapter 27

MOTHER WOLF

February 2, 1773

Mary alternately slept and dreamed. It was more like drifting in and out of consciousness than sleeping, and the dreams were more like nightmares. In between, she felt a presence, one that calmed and comforted her. It was as if her mother were wrapping her arms around her, protecting her, telling her that it was all a bad dream, everything was going to be back to normal when she woke. As she left the dark, unexplained world of her sleep, she felt like what the bear must feel after waking from a winter of hibernation. She was groggy, confused, and she was unsure how long she had been out, but she knew she was hungry and that her body hurt all over.

The female wolf was watching her as Mary woke, but it made no sound. Even in her weakened state, Mary was aware of her surroundings and knew she was not alone in the cave. She had been so exhausted when she reached the cave the night before that she was not aware the she-wolf had followed her up the trail to the cave and made sure Mary was safe inside.

Now the she-wolf lay close to Mary, as if guarding her. As Mary opened her eyes, she found herself looking into the eyes of the large, silver-gray wolf, one that could easily have killed her. Mary was not afraid though. She had seen the wolf on Mohan's Run on more than one occasion and had told the men hunting there not to kill her. They had become friends in the latter part of her pregnancy when the she-wolf would come by her cabin, as if to check up on the mother-to-be, when Charles or her father was away. There was something special about this wolf; Mary knew it the first time she saw her, and she knew their lives were going to be intertwined somehow.

People didn't understand Mary or her abilities, at least not at first, but after knowing her and witnessing the strange happenings that occurred when she was around, it became easier for them to accept what they saw, even if it was hard to believe. Mary's father, Michael, was used to seeing his daughter befriend wild animals, but it took the Mohans a year to even admit that she somehow communicated with all animals. Old Man Eeds himself was strange, so he took to Mary right off and even helped her cultivate her unique talents. Simon Kenton couldn't get past her looks long enough to appreciate her other gifts until right before he took off to Kentucky.

The wolf leaned over to lick Mary's face, a sign of acceptance that brought Mary's thoughts back to the present. She was thankful for the warmth the wolf's fur was bringing to her cold body, but even more than the warmth, she felt loved and cared for. The reality of the past few days sank in as she remembered why she was here in this cave: she was gathering her strength to avenge her family's deaths.

Just then the wolf quickly got up and left the cave. Mary needed to stretch her legs and relieve herself, so she too went outside. The sun was warm upon her skin, with just a little coolness in the slight breeze that brushed past her face. She heard rustling in the bushes to the left of the cave and saw the wolf appear with a rabbit between its teeth. The wolf looked at Mary as if to say, "I caught your breakfast," and entered the cave. Mary followed behind her and watched as the wolf deposited the limp rabbit on Mary's bedding. They understood each other without words. Mary thanked the wolf, extending her hand. The wolf came to her gently, as if she knew Mary was in pain, and nudged her arm with her cold nose. The two played on the cave floor, and then Mary announced that she would build a fire to cook the rabbit.

There were pieces of kindling stacked near the cave entrance from when Mary used to come here in what seemed like a different lifetime. She had her fire-starting kit in her bundle and quickly retrieved it. A flame caught on the dry wood on the first strike and she quickly had the rabbit skinned and roasted on sticks. It smelled so good, and Mary was hungry. She took some water first, knowing that her stomach hadn't had food in days, and she didn't want to be sick. She had a few small vegetables that she roasted in the fire. This was going to be a feast, but first she must give thanks to Grandfather.

Mary gave thanks for her blessings, this cave, the she-wolf, and her food. She wanted more than anything to make her way to her Shawnee uncle's village and seek justice for the deaths of her father, husband, and son, but she realized she was still too weak.

As Mary filled her belly, she tried to think logically about how she would go about getting revenge for the three deaths. It was the middle of winter, and the cold and snow, along with her weakened state, would make traveling difficult. She needed to gain her strength back. At least here in the cave, she had shelter, fresh water, enough small game in the area, and she could build a fire. By spring she would be physically ready to make the journey and deal with her enemy.

Chapter 28

MON DIEU

March 1773

Young Mary heard the shot, then the mournful yelp of the wolf who had been hit by the hunter's long rifle. She knew that even the most experienced hunter could not get another shot off in less than ten to twenty seconds, hopefully enough time for her to get to the man and stop him from killing the wolf she knew was in his trap. A knowing fear rose in her chest, a fear she couldn't dispel. She had not seen her wolf friend, the one she called Mother Wolf, in two days. It was not like her; the she-wolf was seldom gone from her more than four or five hours at a time.

Mary knew men had been trapping wolves in the area, and she couldn't bear the thought of her wolf being the one in the trap. She also knew the she-wolf was pregnant and had left to dig her den in preparation for her pups' births. Mary had made the decision to delay her journey until the she-wolf delivered her pups and raised them to the age they could fend for themselves. This postponed her trip to Red Hawk's camp, but at the same time, it gave her more time to regain her strength.

Mary sensed that the strong spirit of the wolf would keep her alive long enough for her to intervene on the wolf's behalf. She reached for her knife as she raced through the forest she now called her home. She hadn't seen a white man in weeks, not since leaving Mohan's Camp in the middle of the night. And if the truth were known, she wasn't looking forward to meeting this one. She preferred the Indians now to the whites; at least with them she knew where she stood. Most white men didn't care about Earth Mother or her creatures, just about the money they could get from destroying both.

She must have been a frightful sight to the man as she appeared out of nowhere, wielding the knife her Shawnee uncle had given her, her long red curls flying behind her as she ran, her clothing nothing more than a breechcloth, leggings, and a small piece of buckskin to cover her ample breasts. She'd had more encounters than she would like to remember with this kind of man, one who takes but never gives back, one who considers her Shawnee family less than human, savages that were meant to be wiped out like the buffalo.

She could hear the growling of the big wolf as the man prepared to shoot it again. What a coward he was. The poor animal was caught in a trap with no way to retreat, and this useless slug was going to fill it full of holes, out of spite, and discard the carcass to boot. The white man could learn things from her Shawnee brothers about respecting the Great Spirit and all the gifts given to us for our use. Mary heard herself let out a scream as she simultaneously realized it was her wolf in the trap. She flew, trying to knock the gun from the hands of the large, red-faced man. Just as soon as her foot hit his arm, he pulled the trigger, but the force of the young woman's body pushed the muzzle off target just as the powder exploded, sending the ball into the bark of a large oak tree. The man cursed in French and reached for his knife, then realized his adversary was a woman. "Mon Dieu" was all he could say.

Mary realized this was the Frenchman she had beaten in a contest two years ago at the Mohans' camp. Things could not be any worse. Her one friend was wounded by a bullet and stuck in a trap and this man, who was not an honorable man, still held a grudge for the humiliation he felt for letting a woman beat him. Mary knew it was futile, but she tried reasoning with him at first. She had learned his language a couple of years ago when a French trapper stayed with her father for one season.

The Frenchman, however, was not to be reasoned with. He didn't seem to have the wolf on his mind now at all. The dirty man licked his lips, and a smile came across his toothless face as he thought about the more valuable prize he now had in his possession—or at least thought he had. He knew she could shoot better than most men, but he did not know what she was capable of doing, especially in a life and death situation such as this. He had no way of knowing that he faced not just a woman but a woman who would give him a fight he was not prepared for.

Mary knew his kind and what he would do to her if given the chance. She wanted no part of this one but was now forced into battle. He outweighed her by at least a hundred pounds but was fat and, no doubt, slow. He just kept grinning and licking his lips as his eyes never left her breasts. At least he was giving her time to look for an opening. She waited for him to make his move; it was to her advantage to fight defensively and not attack. Attacking would only give her opponent the advantage, and she needed all the advantage she could get now. No, she would wait for him to make his move and then strike a blow. Although he knew she was gifted when it came to her abilities with a gun or bow and arrows, he would not be expecting such a small woman to be so strong or brave. Or was she crazy, as some of the white women near Mohan's Camp had said.

They had never seen a woman do the things she did. It had saved her life more than once, and now she was hoping it would again.

Finally, he came at her, but only after putting his gun down. He wanted both hands free to explore her body no doubt. She didn't think he had seen the sharp blade now at her side. If he had, he would have been more cautious. She knew what she had to do: let him touch her, fondle her, and think he was going to have her naked body at his mercy at any moment. Then, when his guard was down, she would drive her blade as deeply as she could into his disgusting fat belly.

His hot breath was in her face, his unwashed body within inches of hers. The odor was almost more than she could stand, it nearly made her heave, but she prayed to the Great Spirit to help her find the strength and courage to do what she now knew she would have to do—kill this man.

It was over quickly but not before the swine ripped the small buckskin cover from her chest, exposing her large milky-white breasts with the ripe pink nipples. He grabbed her breasts, squeezing them so hard she thought they would come off in his hands. She held her breath as his lips found her left nipple, causing it to become erect as he began sucking on it. He tried pushing her to the ground at the same time that his hands tore at her soft breasts. She knew that if he got on top of her, she would have less chance to drive the knife into him with a killing blow, so she plunged it in as he lifted his face to smile at her, the spit dripping from his chin like a mad dog. His face changed from ecstasy to puzzlement, then pain, and then the knowing truth that he would die. She was as good with her blade as she was her rifle or bow. He wouldn't let go of her, though, as he fell toward the earth, and she thought she had failed in her attack. She had not. He was mortally wounded but fell on her just the same. As she felt the ground beneath her, his fingers loosened, and she managed to break free.

She quickly looked at the wolf to see how it was, and when satisfied her friend could wait another minute, she stepped over the bloated man's back, lifted his head with one hand, and with the other quickly sliced his throat from ear to ear as she had seen her warrior friends do. She wanted to make sure this one was dead and could do no more harm. She then turned her attention to the female wolf, which was still in the white man's trap, blood surrounding her broken leg. Fortunately, the fat Frenchman was not a good shot, and his ball had only nicked the right leg, the one not in the trap. It was the leg in the trap that Mary was worried about. She had to get the wolf out and try to put medicine on the wolf, medicine she had been given by her adopted Shawnee aunt.

Mary began talking to her wolf friend, slowly and softly, as she fought the tears that ran down her cheeks. She did not want to lose this creature, the one that had saved her life. The wolf loved Mary as much as Mary loved the wolf. It was if the two communicated non-verbally, understanding each other with ease. Mary had always been able to feel what the animals were feeling and make them understand her. She wasn't sure herself how she did it, but she did.

She found a large stick to keep the jaws of the trap pried open as she tried to gently remove the wolf's left hind leg. The leg was broken but not severed. She thought she could help her if the wolf allowed her to put medicine on the leg, wrap it, and somehow splint it. Mary was good at what she did, and the wolf knew it as she allowed Mary to pull her injured leg from the steel trap and tend to it as gently as any mother would her child. After Mary was done, she offered the great female wolf some of her food and water, and they left the camp of the dead man for the mile-long trip downstream to their cave. Mary wanted to carry the wolf but thought she might be pushing her luck, so she walked slowly, encouraging the animal all the way.

As they walked away, Mary turned to take one last look at the dead Frenchman. She smiled when she saw the buzzards were already making a meal of his fat carcass. He didn't deserve a burial. He was getting what he deserved.

Partway down the trail, the she-wolf paused, looked at Mary, and began to whine. Mary was afraid this was all too much for her wolf friend that was in pain and possibly dying. The wolf looked at Mary as if pleading and turned off the path toward the hill.

Mary followed, and it was soon clear why the wolf wanted to go this way. She had a den, and no doubt had fought the Frenchman as he tried to kill her pups. When they reached the den, Mary fell to her knees, crying out in pain and anger. Before her she saw what was left of the she-wolf's pups: five were lying on the ground, cut and butchered. The sixth one, the only one alive, poked his head out of the den and cried for his mother. The she-wolf slowly made her way to her son and placed herself so that he could suckle her breast. Mary could only imagine the ferocity of Mother Wolf and how she had fought for her life and the lives of her pups.

While the pup was satisfying his hunger, Mary picked up each dead wolf pup and said a prayer over it as she placed it inside their den. She found large rocks nearby and wedged them into the opening of the den, then used her strong legs to kick the rocks tightly into the opening to, hopefully, prevent any scavengers getting to the small bodies.

Once the sole surviving pup had nursed his fill, the three made their way to Mary's cave. It took the better part of an hour for them to get there. Mary walked slowly, carrying the pup as Mother Wolf kept pace with her. The cave was partway up a hill, covered well by the forest and hidden from the path they were on. She hesitated to light a fire in case there were other white men in the area, but she knew it was needed to keep her friend and the pup warm so she built a small one. One thing Old Man Eeds had shown her was a second opening in the top of the cave farther back from the front entrance. The smoke was drawn out that opening, helping to hide the exact location of the cave.

After making sure they had water, Mother Wolf had food, and both mother and pup were comfortable, Mary curled up by the fire and quickly fell asleep. Something woke her in the middle of the night: a warm, wet thing on her face. She recoiled and was ready to strike but stopped when she realized it was the female wolf and her pup licking her face. She gently stroked them both, telling them how brave they were, how she would take care of them, and protect them with her life. Mary put her face to the she-wolf's face and thanked the Creator for His gift of life and these two magnificent creatures.

At that moment Mary decided to call the pup Brother Wolf. She told him as she stroked his soft fur. It fit. They all fell asleep, not waking until the sun had been up for over an hour.

Chapter 29

SPIRIT WARRIOR

July 1773

The young woman's breath came in deep gasps as she assessed her situation, and she could feel that all-too-familiar heat rising from inside her body, the heat she felt when danger threatened her. The fine, blonde hair stood up on her arms, and her hearing became acute as she listened to the three men before her. Beside her campfire stood three Indians, obviously discussing her immediate future. Beside her was the male wolf, the one she called Brother Wolf, the lone survivor of Mother Wolf's litter, the only one she could save from the Frenchman. That day seemed like a lifetime ago as she stood on the softly carpeted ground of the dark forest just as the sun was disappearing in the west.

Mary quickly realized that one of the Indians was Digging Turtle, the man she saw in her nightmares, the one who killed her beloved Charles. At first she didn't pay too much attention to the other two men; all she could think about was killing her enemy. He might remember her, but it had been years since he had seen her. She had the advantage of knowing what he looked like now, not just remembering him as a young man. She thought she knew the other two warriors. One was tall and looked very strong, and the third looked to be a good many years older than his companions. She had met the two of them when visiting Walking Owl's camp ten years ago. They, in turn, were paying more attention to Digging Turtle than to her.

Mary listened to their conversation as she also tried to keep her four-legged friend, the one she called her brother, from attacking the man who seemed hell bent on causing her more pain. She whispered to the wolf to be quiet, to stay where he was, but it was becoming more difficult every second, as she could feel his hot breath on her leg and see his white fangs bared in the threatening manner she had seen so many times before when they hunted together. She knew she could only control this wild animal so long because he was just that, a wild animal and not a pet to be dominated by his master. Besides, he fiercely loved her and would give his life for her, as she would for him. She didn't want to think about either one of those possibilities right now. She had to decide what her plan of action was going to be, depending on what the three men just inside her firelight did.

The Indian closest to her, the tallest of the three, seemed kind, as did the older warrior. From what she could make out of their conversation, they just wanted to share her fire, her food, and be on their way. Despite her dread of what would certainly happen in the next few minutes, the lean and muscular woman couldn't keep her eyes off the tallest one. He was the one who kept drawing her attention away from Digging Turtle. She felt guilty thinking about him as she had thought of Charles. She imagined him touching her skin, pressing his lips on hers. *Stop it!* she said in her head. She should not be having these thoughts. She still loved Charles and always would.

She tried to hang onto the Indians' every word so that, with luck, she would be prepared for what was to follow. The three men before her couldn't know that she spoke their language, at least enough to understand that she was in more danger than she had been since killing the Frenchman.

In what seemed like an eternity, but was only two or three minutes, the men had gone from a quiet discussion on the fate of the beautiful young woman with red hair and flashing green eyes to yelling at each other about what should be done with the woman and the wolf. Digging Turtle, the one with hatred in his eyes, finally turned away from the other two as if to walk away back into the darkness of the forest night. She thought the one with the kind eyes had been the victor in this verbal battle, but suddenly, Digging Turtle turned back around, his right hand grasping a long blade that shimmered in the firelight, his eyes wide with lustful anticipation of what was soon to be his. His mouth opened and he was just beginning to let out the blood-curdling scream she had heard once before when her wolf brother leapt in the air to intercept the attacker. But Mary was also quick and managed to insert herself between the wolf and the man.

She knew Digging Turtle would kill her beloved friend first and then turn his attention to her. She thought she could almost endure him assaulting her, but the thought of losing her friend gave her even more courage and determination than usual. Just as all three were about to collide, she grabbed his outstretched arms, planted one foot in his groin, and rolled onto her back, using her leverage to throw him over her head onto the ground. She knew her move could be dangerous, as her wild wolf brother was also making his own attack and she could get hurt in the process, but it would be worth it if she could distract her enemy long enough to reach her own weapon. In the three seconds it took for the wild-eyed Indian to turn, pull his knife, and advance toward her, the other one, the tallest one, also began making his move in her direction.

They all four seemed to reach the same point at the same time— Digging Turtle, his companion, the young woman, and the wolf. Fangs reached to tear at the evil one's throat as the soft yet strong arms of the young woman reached out for her attacker's arms as he raised his knife to strike at her beloved brother, the wolf that was now ready to give his life for her. It all happened as if slow motion. The scream burst forth from the evil one's lips as his right hand raised even higher for the strike that was to fall upon the silvery coat of the wolf that was two feet in the air now, inches from the throat of the one he wanted to kill. Mary's strong arms reached their mark as she grabbed the muscular arms of the man before her, but at the same time another set of arms—the arms of the man who made her feel uncomfortable yet, at the same time, almost safe—reached for her.

The collision jarred her head and sent the breath from her body. She managed to get her foot on its target, but the arms of the other man pulled her off balance as she was about to execute the technique she had done a hundred times as a girl learning how to defend herself in this wild country. Her adopted Indian family had taught her well, and even with the force pulling her to her right, she managed to push on the wolf just enough with her left hip to send him out of the reach of the knife.

Now all four were in motion, tumbling through the night air as if weightless. She knew she had to recover quickly and pull her own knife because she knew the warrior she had sent flying was going to be angry that a mere woman had pulled this old trick on him. What she hadn't counted on was the taller one pulling his knife—not on her but on his companion. With one hand he pushed her to his left, and with the other already holding his gleaming knife, he was on top of Digging Turtle before he had a chance to find the blade that had been knocked from his grip just seconds ago. The third warrior, an older man, stood watching over the taller one as if protecting his chief.

Mary's first thought was for her brother wolf. He had ended up on the opposite side of their campsite, fifteen feet away from where she stood. But he was already on his feet and going after the two men struggling on the ground. She yelled to him to stop in the native language she had been taught just as he reached the right arm of the one who was trying to save them. She feared for both their lives and screamed again. This not only halted the wolf's advance but the fight between the two Indians as well. Mary realized this was the first sound that had come out of her mouth since the three men had entered her camp. Brother Wolf quickly came to her side, greeting her in the same way a wolf would greet another wolf of equal rank in his pack. Both men stood up and looked at her and the wolf in amazement. She didn't know what shocked them more, the fact she could speak their language or the fact she could speak the wolf's language.

The taller one grabbed Digging Turtle and told him to leave, to go back to his village and he and White Elk would be there soon to talk to Red Hawk. The evil one glared at her with his dark eyes as he brushed past her and the wolf. The move caused the wolf to emit a low guttural growl again.

It was all Mary could do to keep her wolf friend from resuming his attack. She began speaking softly to him, like a mother trying to comfort her child. She glared back at the evil one as if to tell him that she was not afraid of him—or any man. In her heart she knew she should be very afraid of him, that she had not heard the last of him, and that he would someday try to kill her again. What he didn't know was that she was here to kill him.

She had immediately known it was him when the three warriors appeared from the forest. It was a feeling that crept over her, and sometimes, pictures came to her head when she felt that way. It had saved her life before, and she knew it would again.

Within seconds, the one with the evil eyes was gone, and she was left alone with her male wolf companion and the two warriors. They all three stood looking at each other in silence. Then the tall man spoke softly to her in his language. "My name is Spirit Warrior, this is White Elk," he said. "What is your name?"

The Irish lass felt her mouth go dry as she tried to answer him. Now she knew who he was: the son of Walking Owl. She spoke softly at first, and very slowly, thinking about every word before she allowed it to escape into the now cool night air. She told him her name was Mary Ryan and that she had traveled with her father, Michael Ryan, from Ireland in 1762. She knew he was going to ask about the wolf and how she knew his language, but she was not going to offer too much information too quickly. She was going to make him ask each question, giving her time to take in the beauty of his body as she spoke.

Mary told him, when he finally asked, that the wolf did not belong to her, that he was wild. She had saved him and his mother when a hunter had shot the great silver-colored male's mother after trapping her, wounding her in the leg, and Mary nursed them back to health. She had called the she-wolf Mother Wolf and her pup

Brother Wolf. Unfortunately, Mother Wolf had never fully recovered from her injuries and had recently died.

The warrior stood looking at the small woman, in awe not only of her beauty and her body but in her abilities as well. She was as good as any warrior in his village at hand-to-hand combat, cunning and quick, and she had the ability to communicate with her wolf friend. The animal stood close to her, his eyes never leaving the man's body. Spirit Wolf smiled then said to Mary, "You must be Sister Wolf then!"

Mary smiled. She liked that and agreed. It was a fine name for her.

Spirit Warrior knew enough not to look the wolf directly in the eyes, as that would be perceived as a direct threat. Anyway, he preferred to gaze upon the marvelous female creature before him. He was becoming more aware of her feminine qualities and of his obvious attraction to her as the moments wore on. Spirit Warrior then asked her how it was that she had come to learn his language.

Once again the red-headed woman chose her words carefully as she explained about her life in Ireland before traveling to this country with her father after her mother's death. She explained how her father, Michael Ryan, had made his way westward toward the now-famous land of "Kain-tuck-ee" in hopes of getting a piece of land of his own. They stayed in a place in western Virginia called Mohan's Camp with the Mohan brothers for a year before Mary and her father were captured by some Shawnee and taken to their village across the Ohio River. There they met a kind chief, Red Hawk, who befriended them and took an instant liking to the young girl. At this point the warrior had a smile on his face and

Mary realized she had told him more than she had intended. She quickly finished her story by just adding the fact that Red Hawk adopted her father after he ran the gauntlet.

Spirit Warrior now remembered who she was. He remembered catching a glimpse of her red hair as she and her adopted uncle passed by him on their way into the encampment. He thought back to the night when his uncle, Red Hawk, introduced his adopted brother and the man's daughter to the people of his village.

Mary politely asked both warriors if they would like food or water and began acting as a hostess, at the same time not wanting to take her eyes off Spirit Warrior's chest. She wondered how it would feel to lay her head on it at night, how those arms would feel encircling her body, how his lips would feel against hers as the two people explored each other in passion. She felt a warm feeling come over her again, not the one she had felt with danger but the one she had felt when she first tasted the sweetness of her beloved Charles McLain's body. She felt a twinge of guilt as she imagined herself with another man. Try as she might, she couldn't get those feelings out of her head or her body. The warrior's closeness excited her more as she tried to concentrate on what she was doing. She hoped the warrior could not tell by her face what she was thinking about or by the aroma her body gave off that meant she was "ready." It had been a long time since she had felt a man's body on top of hers or the impatient pressing of his hips against hers as she fumbled to be free of her clothing.

White Elk ate quickly then said he would go to Red Hawk's camp to announce their arrival. He would travel with Red Hawk to Walking Owl's camp, where the matter of Digging Turtle would be settled. Mary and Spirit Warrior ate in silence, both lost in their thoughts, thoughts that were not at all unlike. He asked her to go with him to his village—as his guest, not his captive—for a celebration. She would be honored for her bravery and ability as a warrior.

It would be great to see Red Hawk, White Feather, and Walking Owl again. Mary said she would go on one condition—that he promise that her brother, the wolf, would not be harmed in any way. She knew she could not keep the wolf from following her into the village and wanted to be sure he would be safe. When Spirit Warrior assured her that no harm would come to the wolf, Mary got that feeling again, the one that told her she was headed for danger, but this man before her seemed worth any danger she might face.

Mary explained that she needed to see her uncle, Red Hawk. It was an urgent matter. Spirit Warrior said that he and White Elk had been on their way to Red Hawk's camp with Digging Turtle. He had been disobeying the chiefs and had gone on an individual killing spree and was to face punishment. Although Mary was glad to hear his behavior was not approved of by Red Hawk or Walking Owl, she nevertheless had a burning desire to punish him herself. Mary did not share this fact with Spirit Warrior. She was not ready.

Chapter 30

THE REUNION

July 1773

As the young woman and her warrior friend walked in the lush green woods toward his village, both were lost in their own thoughts. The Irish lass was thinking of her homeland, Ireland, and how long ago and far away it seemed. This land reminded her of the land she loved so much across the great water, yet it was different. Ireland seemed so old and tired compared to this land called Virginia. Yet these hills gave her the same safe feeling she'd had when she was a young lass running wild in the fields just below the ancient Rock of Cashel. She had loved to spend the entire day alone, except for her animal friends, just dreaming of the man she would marry someday.

With this thought, she quickly returned to the present and then thought how she had never pictured herself back then with a man such as the one now walking beside her—but she certainly did now.

The warrior was also thinking of the past, of how he had once loved a Shawnee maiden, She is Favored, who had died in childbirth along with his infant son. Spirit Warrior felt a sharp pain in his chest as he thought of the loss of his wife and child. It had been two years, but the wound was still not healed. He wondered what she would think of his feelings for this woman. He quickly pushed these thoughts aside, in guilt mostly, because he had not let himself think about such things since her death. Just then a cool, soft breeze caressed his naked chest, and he thought he heard a voice, yet he could not make out what it said. He looked at the young Irish girl and knew she could hear it too.

He looked around and noticed there was no movement in the trees above him to show any wind. Then he saw it: a beautiful butterfly, just like the one he had seen after the ceremony when his wife and son died. It flew around him in a circle, just like that day, as if to say, "It is I, your wife, and we are with you now and forever." He couldn't understand how he knew this; he just did. He looked at the young woman beside him and saw that she too had noticed the butterfly. They stopped in their tracks as the beautiful, multi-colored creature gracefully danced around Spirit Warrior, then around the woman he called Sister Wolf, then widened its circle to include them both. Spirit Warrior knew deep down what that meant; he just wasn't ready to accept it yet.

Both the man and the woman stood still until the butterfly had finished its dance and flew off into the woods. Neither one spoke for what seemed like an eternity. Both knew something important had just happened and were trying to understand its meaning. Finally, the warrior spoke. "I think this is a good spot to rest awhile and eat something before going on." It would be at least four more hours of difficult walking before they reached his village, and he welcomed another chance to just sit and look at the face of this magnificent woman.

Mary also welcomed the chance to sit on the Earth Mother she had come to love so much since living with the Shawnee. She was more Indian now than white. She really didn't care if she ever saw another white man if she could spend the rest of her days with the man now by her side.

They ate in silence. Both were a little uncomfortable to be alone with each other for the first time, although neither knew the other one had similar thoughts. It would have been so much easier if they just talked to one another, but that was not to be. Both were proud and stubborn and not used to having to think about other people's feelings.

The rest of the journey was uneventful until just before reaching the outskirts of the village. White Elk had made his way back earlier and delivered the message of the chief's son's arrival with the strange white woman. The entire village was filled with excitement in anticipation of their arrival, and a feast was being prepared by the women of the village. The chief was looking forward to seeing his son but also to meeting the woman. He had a feeling he knew who she was from White Elk's description.

Red Hawk and White Feather had made the journey to Walking Owl's camp along with other warriors. There would be a council to decide the fate of Digging Turtle. He had been confined in a wigwam, and a warrior was assigned to guard him. As Red Hawk and Walking Owl sat to discuss what they knew they would have to do, a familiar voice called their names. They both stood up to see Mary running down the path that led to the village, a silver-gray wolf at her side.

"Uncles!" Mary embraced White Feather, Red Hawk, then Walking Owl. They were glad to see each other; it had been a long time. Mary sat between the two chiefs and told her story. She had married Charles and was pregnant with his son when Charles, the baby, and Mary's father, Michael, all died the same day due to Digging Turtle.

Spirit Warrior listened intently to what she said, and he now understood her better; they shared a similar history. Red Hawk was deeply saddened to hear of his brother's death and of the death of Mary's husband and baby. He was angry that Charles had died at the hands of one of his own warriors. Red Hawk explained that a council would be called the next day, and the warriors would decide what to do about Digging Turtle.

Mary took a deep breath, then pulled the wrapped articles from her bag. The knife and medicine bag belonging to Digging Turtle brought so much pain to her heart that she could barely touch them. It took a minute for her to be able to speak. "Uncles, I have come to you to seek justice for my family. This is the knife that killed my husband. This medicine bag was torn from the neck of the man who killed Charles."

Both Red Hawk and Walking Owl knew the two items belonged to Digging Turtle.

Mary continued. "My father was not guilty of killing Digging Turtle's father and uncle for no reason, he was simply defending himself. My husband, Charles, had nothing to do with anyone's death, yet he died for no reason except hate."

No one could say a word for a minute after hearing Mary's plea. Finally, Red Hawk spoke first. "Mary, we are sorry for what you and your family have gone through."

Walking Owl added, "There is no honor in what Digging Turtle has done. He will be punished."

Mary was relieved to hear the words from the two great chiefs. White Feather hugged Mary and offered to wrap the two items of death in the cloth and put them away. Mary thanked her, but she wrapped them herself and placed them back in her bag.

The women announced that the feast was ready. While everyone was eating, Spirit Warrior told his father and uncle about what had happened when they had first come upon Mary's camp. Even though White Elk had already explained about Digging Turtle's attack on Mary, all listened intently as Spirit Warrior explained Mary's bravery and her ability to fight the larger man. Brother Wolf sat quietly at Mary's side as Spirit Warrior bragged about the wolf's bravery also and his love for Mary. It was then that he announced Mary's new name: Sister Wolf. All nodded in agreement.

Chapter 31

A FITTING END

July 1773

After the feast the villagers retired to their wigwams. Spirit Warrior and Walking Owl told Mary goodnight first and strolled to their wigwams. Red Hawk and White Feather were guests, as was Mary, and they were placed in wigwams close to the center of camp. White Feather asked if she and the wolf wanted to stay with them, knowing how difficult the past couple of days had been, but Mary graciously refused. She didn't want Brother Wolf to keep them up. The three embraced then Mary walked to her wigwam. She settled in and put her things away.

When the wolf looked at her with the look she knew meant he had to go outside, she let him out the opening then turned to finish her bed. It was no more than a minute later that she heard him growl. It upset her as she knew it meant only one thing: Digging Turtle was close by. She reached into her bag, and when she did, the knife and medicine bag fell to the ground. She quickly picked up the knife and ran outside.

Brother Wolf stood near her wigwam, the silver hair on his back standing straight up. Digging Turtle was coming toward her and there was no one else in sight. He struck at her with a toma-hawk just as she was going to strike him with his own knife and her brother, the wolf, was jumping for the evil one's throat. Mary was able to block the tomahawk with her left arm and managed to thrust the knife up and into the soft area below Digging Turtle's breastbone. There was blood everywhere, all of it from Digging Turtle.

All the noise drew a few warriors, including Red Hawk, Walking Owl, and Spirit Warrior, who yelled for Digging Turtle to stop. Stop he did, looking at Mary in disbelief, not wanting to admit defeat at the hands of a woman. Mary screamed at him, telling him he had caused her so much pain, and now he would pay the price. Before Spirit Warrior could get to her, she pulled the knife from his abdomen and began stabbing him in the throat. As if Brother Wolf knew she was the victor, he stayed close to her but didn't attack the warrior.

Spirit Warrior reached Mary first, just as Digging Turtle fell to the ground. She was oblivious to everyone there; her attention was still on her enemy. Brother Wolf nudged her leg, getting her attention. She bent down to hug the wolf and began to cry for the first time in months. Red Hawk and Walking Owl checked Digging Turtle, who was dead. Spirit Warrior could only stand silently by as he watched Mary and her wolf. Finally, the red-haired lass looked up directly into the eyes of Spirit Warrior, who had tears in his eyes. She stood facing him as he placed his hands on her shoulders. He admired her so much, not just for her beauty, but for her strength and bravery. She must have loved Charles deeply. Spirit Warrior wondered if she could love anyone else that much again. He hoped so. Mary noticed the tears in her admirer's eyes and understood their meaning. They both had loved and lost. She thanked him for coming to her aid and for defending her. He pulled her closer to him and they embraced, then turned their attention to the man lying on the ground.

Red Hawk announced to the now larger group of people standing nearby that Digging Turtle was dead. There would be no need for a council to meet to determine his fate. Mary explained to Red Hawk that she had found Digging Turtle outside her wigwam and had defended herself when he attacked her with a tomahawk.

Walking Owl asked, "Is there anyone here that doubts Mary's actions were anything but in defense of her life?" No one came forward to dispute Mary's claims.

Red Wing came from the wigwam where Digging Turtle had been held to announce that the warrior who had been guarding him needed attention. Somehow, Digging Turtle had managed to overpower the warrior, take his tomahawk, and split his skull with it, before running toward Mary.

Mary quickly grabbed her bundle and ran to the fallen warrior. The group watched in amazement as she assessed his situation, pulled items from her bundle, and began to take care of him. She applied pressure to the wound first, then cleaned it. She knew what to use to slow down the bleeding, then bandaged his head and helped settle him in the wigwam. Everyone who witnessed her actions thought the same thing: she was as good as any medicine man they had ever known. Not only was she physically capable of defending herself as well as any warrior in camp, but she also had the ability and knowledge to take care of others in need.

Spirit Warrior noticed his father and Red Hawk talking quietly on the side and waited respectfully until they noticed him then motioned for him to come to them. In his heart he knew what the conversation was about. The group should make Mary a warrior. Instead of the council tomorrow deciding Digging Turtle's fate, it would be a council of warriors deciding whether to accept another warrior into their group.

Walking Owl asked his son what was on his mind, and Spirit Warrior said, "Father, I think Mary Sister Wolf should be a warrior. I would like for you to call a council tomorrow to ask the other warriors to accept her."

Both Red Hawk and Walking Owl smiled at the younger man. He was wise and would someday become a chief himself. The three men discussed it briefly, then turned their attention to Mary while two of the warriors picked up the body of Digging Turtle to take it out of camp.

Red Hawk insisted that Mary spend the night in his wigwam with White Feather. Even though he knew the danger was over, he thought she could use the companionship of his beloved wife. Mary, not wanting to be any more trouble to her uncle, politely said no. Spirit Wolf suggested that his uncle, Red Hawk, use his wigwam, and he would stay outside his uncle's, guarding the two women for the night. Red Hawk and Walking Owl both smiled again at the younger man. They were both pleased that he was finally showing an interest in another woman after losing his wife and son two years before.

Since Digging Turtle had brought shame to his village, the normal burial practice of cleansing his body, having a ceremony to honor his bravery, and showing him respect in the afterlife would not be done. He had no living relatives to perform the cleansing ritual. The two warriors would find some skins to wrap the body in and, at daybreak, find a place in the woods to dig a shallow grave. There would be no one there to mourn his death. *It is a fitting end for the evil one,* Mary thought.

Chapter 32

THE VISIT

July 1773

The day after the death of Digging Turtle, the warrior council accepted Mary as a warrior. She was honored with an owl feather and all the warriors were proud to have her as a warrior. Red Hawk also officially gave her the name "Sister Wolf." Spirit Warrior smiled and was happy that she accepted both honors, being a warrior and her new name.

The next few months Mary Sister Wolf and Brother Wolf were comfortable in Red Hawk's village. She had settled into her daily routine, spending time with Brother Wolf and participating in hunts with the warriors. Even though she hated to kill the beautiful animals, it was part of being a warrior, and she must be able to provide for the people of her village. Spirit Warrior spent more time in his uncle's village than his own. It took Mary some time to be open to a new relationship, as she felt guilty about it, feeling as if she were betraying Charles. One night, after spending time with Spirit Warrior around the fire with the other warriors, she had trouble sleeping. Her thoughts were on Charles and their son, Ryan. As she drifted off to sleep, she felt a presence in her wigwam. She opened her eyes to see Charles kneeling beside her. Brother Wolf didn't make a sound.

"Charles!" Mary said aloud. He put his finger to her lips, as he had done before. She didn't have to speak; it was as if they heard each other's thoughts. "I have missed you so much. Where's Ryan? How is it that you are here?"

"I have missed you too. Ryan is with your parents. I am here to tell you that I am always with you. I watch over you."

Mary hung her head in shame. This meant that Charles had seen her with Spirit Warrior.

"Look at me."

Mary looked up into the blue eyes of her husband, the same blue eyes that she had become lost in every time she looked into them since the first day they had met.

"I will always love you, and I know that you will always love me. Spirit Warrior loves you too, and he needs you as much as you need him. Be happy, lass, enjoy your time here. We will see each other again, but for now you must not live in the past."

Mary closed her eyes; tears began running down her cheeks. When she opened her eyes again, Charles was gone. "Wait! Come back!" Brother Wolf nudged her arm and curled up beside her as she cried herself to sleep.

The next day Mary went to speak to White Feather, explaining her dream from the night before. White Feather listened and waited for Mary to finish her story. "My child," White Feather said softly, "you have been given many gifts from the Creator. Be thankful for them. Open your heart, listen to the messages you are given. It is meant to be."

Mary felt better after speaking to her aunt.

Later that day, Spirit Warrior approached his uncle to ask for his blessing. He wanted to make Mary Sister Wolf his wife. Red Hawk replied, "You must give her time to grieve over her losses, just as you have yours. She will know when the time is right. I will be honored to perform the ceremony when she is ready."

The warrior took his uncle's advice. The two young people got to know each other and talked of their pasts, their losses, and finally, their future. The following year Red Hawk performed the Bonding Ceremony for Spirit Warrior and Sister Wolf. During the ceremony, Sister Wolf presented the beaded necklace she had made for her new husband. She placed it over his head, resting it on his strong, muscular chest. The entire village erupted into enthusiastic cheering for the young couple. They both hoped the two could help influence a peaceful agreement between their peoples. Mary Sister Wolf knew it would be difficult. She knew the winds of war were blowing in their direction again.

Chapter 33

THE WINDS OF WAR

1774 – 1776

Simon Girty visited the Shawnee villages of Red Hawk and Walking Owl often. The news he brought was difficult for the two men to accept. The white renegade spoke of political dealings of the British across the great water. They still had control over most of the land that once was considered the Shawnees, and the white settlers were rebelling against them.

Girty explained that he had counseled with several of the chiefs from various tribes. They all said the same thing. Early in the disputes between the colonists and the British, they had tried to figure out which side would be in the best position to protect their land. Some believed it was in their best interest to remain neutral. Others stated there was no guarantee that remaining neutral would be respected by either side.

The tensions continued to grow, and Simon Girty was in the middle. He had lived with Guyasuta, chief of the Ohio Seneca, and had recently visited him. They discussed the many battles they had fought against the British in the French and Indian War and of their alliance with Pontiac. The old chief had fought at the Siege of Fort Pitt, the Battle of Bloody Run, and the Battle of Bushy Run. He had hoped the fighting was over but was told of the recent battles of Lexington and Concord, which meant the colonists and the British were now at war. His eyes filled with tears as he explained this to his adopted son, Simon Girty. No matter which side won, both men knew the Indians were going to lose much. This was also discussed with Red Hawk and Walking Owl. All three men agreed that no matter which side they allied with, they would not come out winners.

During this time, Mary Sister Wolf and Spirit Warrior started their family while living in Red Hawk's village. Mary gave birth to a son on April 29, 1776. He loudly announced his arrival late that night as White Feather assisted Sister Wolf in her delivery. Spirit Warrior paced outside their wigwam until he heard the first cry of his son, then ran inside to see his red-haired wife holding their son in her right arm. Sister Wolf looked into the eyes of her son, and a calming feeling came over her. She had loved her first husband, Charles, and still mourned his death and the deaths of her first son and her father. But now it was if the Creator spoke to her through her son, saying, "All things happen for a reason." She knew that if her first husband had lived, she would not be holding this baby in her arms. It was the first time in over three years that she did not feel the pain in her heart that had become a constant in her life.

Spirit Warrior was experiencing similar feelings. He too had lost a first love and a baby boy. He would always love his first wife, and mourn the loss of his family, but now he had a new wife and baby. They did not replace what he had lost, and he and the new baby did not replace what Sister Wolf had lost. Both Spirit Warrior and Sister Wolf understood the other's losses and respected what was.

White Feather moved to the other side of Sister Wolf to let Spirit Warrior kneel beside his wife and see his son. He first touched the red hair of his wife, then the darker hair of his son as he announced his new son's name to his wife and White Feather. "When I heard my son cry, I knew that his name should be Lalawethika, He Makes Noise. He will be a great chief one day."

Red Hawk entered the wigwam to see the newest member of his village. He congratulated his nephew, Spirit Warrior, and hugged his niece, Sister Wolf. He gazed at the newborn and agreed with his nephew. "This one is destined to be a great chief." White Feather asked Sister Wolf if she needed anything else, then she and Red Hawk left to give the family some time together.

Spirit Warrior could not stop smiling. He was happy and it showed. He took some tobacco, raised it up, and said a prayer of thanks to the Creator. He couldn't stop looking at his wife and son. His heart was full. He curled up beside them, and for this one night, he tried not to think about what was going on outside his village.

Neither he nor Sister Wolf could push the images of war from their minds in the weeks and months to come. They both knew it would be a part of their future life, but for tonight, they both wanted to just be a family and hope their son would not get caught up in the struggle between Britain and the colonies.

Chapter 34

THE YEAR OF THE BLOODY SEVENS

1777

The year 1777 turned out to be one of the bloodiest years in American History, especially on the western frontier. Simon Girty once again reported to Red Hawk and Walking Owl about the events going on east of their villages in what was being called the American Revolution. The thirteen colonies were trying to break from the King of England, and the British enlisted more help from their allies, the Indians, to harass the American settlers in the west. The British hoped American troops would be diverted from the east to protect the western frontier. General Hamilton, the British commander of Fort Detroit, bought American scalps from the Indians. He provided them with lead, powder, trade muskets, wool blankets, tomahawks, and scalping knives and encouraged them to attack settlers from the Ohio River to the Allegheny Mountains. This proved deadly to all involved.

Spirit Warrior, Sister Wolf, Red Hawk, and Walking Owl listened intently as Girty reported that his friend, Simon (Butler) Kenton, had finally found his way to Kentucky. Mary Sister Wolf was especially delighted to hear of her old friend, but she was sorry he hadn't claimed his true name yet.

In April 1777 Daniel Boone was outside Fort Boonesborough when the Shawnee attacked. Before he could make it to safety, he was struck in the leg with a bullet. Unable to run, he looked up at a warrior ready to strike him with his tomahawk. Fortunately for Boone, Simon Kenton was nearby. Known for his ability to reload on the run, he appeared in time to shoot the attacking warrior and club another one. He picked Boone up in his arms and ran toward the fort. Before reaching the fort, two warriors again attacked them. This time Kenton threw his friend at the warriors, knocking them down. Kenton killed one with a tomahawk, picked up Boone again, and kicked the other Indian in the chest. They made it safely inside the walls of Boonesborough.

Although Boone was praising his friend for his heroic deeds, Simon didn't seem to hear him. The conversation Simon had had with Mary Ryan six years prior was running through his head. Mary had asked him to watch over Daniel Boone, and if he was attacked, he was to throw Daniel at the Indians. "Daniel, throw Daniel at them," was one of the last things Mary said to him before he left Mohan's Camp. How did she know?

Girty told Mary that Boone had said, "Well, Simon, you behaved like a man today. Indeed you are a fine fellow." Mary blushed as Girty mentioned her involvement with Simon Kenton. She looked at Spirit Warrior and he smiled. He knew she had only been trying to help. She had never told him of their kiss, though, and now was not the time to bring it up.

Simon Girty reminded the chiefs of their friend Cornstalk and the Battle of Point Pleasant, which was the only major action of Dunmore's War. It was fought between Virginia militia and Shawnee and Mingo warriors. Shawnee Chief Cornstalk attacked the Virginia militia at Point Pleasant at the confluence of the Ohio and Kanawha rivers. After a long and difficult battle, Cornstalk retreated and was forced to make peace in the Treaty of Camp Charlotte. The Shawnee had to give up their claims to all lands south of the Ohio River.

Cornstalk was a man of his word and abided by the treaty for the rest of his life. The American Revolution had begun and the British needed the help of the Shawnee, who alone had not joined forces with the British. The British urged the Shawnee to drive the white settlers out of the region. The Shawnee, in turn, hoped the British would help them reclaim the lands. The young warriors wanted to avenge those slain at the Battle of Point Pleasant, but Cornstalk opposed the confederacy. He did not want war with "the long knives," as the Virginians were known. He believed the tribe's safety could only be found in friendship with the Virginians. By the winter of 1776, the Shawnee were divided into two factions, one led by Cornstalk, who wanted to remain neutral, and militant bands led by men such as Blue Jacket.

The expression on Girty's face changed to one of concern when he spoke of Cornstalk's recent peace agreement with the white men. He had requested a talk with Captain Arbuckle, the commander of the fort at Point Pleasant. He knew the British were coaxing the Indians to attack and he, a Delaware chief, and another Indian went to the fort to try to negotiate peace before the fighting began.

Captain Arbuckle decided to take the three men hostage. The Americans believed they could use Cornstalk to keep the other tribes from attacking. Two days later, Cornstalk's son, Ellinipisco, came to the fort to see his father, and he was also taken hostage.

Girty put his head down and was slow to relate the end of the story. Three days after Cornstalk arrived at the fort, an American militiaman from the fort was killed nearby by unknown Indians. When the soldier's bloody body was returned to the fort, a group of soldiers, against orders, broke into the quarters where Cornstalk and the other Indians were being held, intent on executing the prisoners. When they burst through the door, Cornstalk rose to meet them. His bravery caused the soldiers to pause momentarily, but then they opened fire.

Cornstalk was shot eight times before he fell to the floor. The other three men were dead. As Cornstalk lay dying on the floor, he said, "I was the border man's friend. Many times I have saved him and his people from harm. I never warred with you, but only wanted to protect our wigwams and lands. I refused to join your paleface enemies with the red coats. I came to the fort as your friend and you murdered me. You have murdered by my side my young son … For this, may the curse of the Great Spirit rest upon this land. May it be blighted by nature. May it even be blighted in its hopes. May the stain of our blood paralyze the strength of its peoples."

While the Revolutionary War waged on in the east, the British used their influence to keep pushing the Indians to attack the Americans, placing bounties on scalps turned in to them. Western Virginia, Pennsylvania, and Kentucky were covered in the blood of the settlers. Kentucky would become known as The Dark and Bloody Ground. The traditional hunting ground of many of the tribes had been invaded by the never-ending procession of men with pale faces. The Indians were seeking revenge, not only for the loss of their hunting grounds but for the deaths of so many of their people. They were fighting a losing battle.

Chapter 35

THE BATTLE OF FALLEN TIMBERS

August 20, 1794

After Spirit Warrior's son, Lalawethika, was born, father and son spent as much time together as possible. The young father knew that his son's way of life would be much different than his had been. Although the British colonists had been here when Spirit Warrior was born, they had not pushed as far west as they were now. There was a never-ending stream of settlers seeking their fortune in the New World. This meant the displacement of the many tribes who had lived or hunted the area for hundreds of years before the first white man set foot on this continent.

Spirit Warrior talked with his son often about what had happened in the past and included him in counsel meetings, hoping his son would become a chief one day. During a recent council, many warriors spoke of the increasing difficulty of remaining neutral while their world crumbled around them. Many of the local tribes pushed back against the onslaught, but it seemed futile. Some had sided with the French in the early days, others with the British. Both the French and the British used the natives to harass settlers, and much blood was shed. Now there was disagreement among the tribes whether to continue to wage war against the whites or to push their people farther west, farther from their homelands and the bodies of their ancestors. This was now Spirit Warrior's problem as he became the chief of his father's village, and like Cornstalk and Nonhelema before him, he advocated for peace. An argument started between Spirit Warrior and Wildcat, who wanted to go to war. Wanting peace and achieving peace were two different things. It seemed to Spirit Warrior that there would never be peace.

Once again, Simon Girty, friend of the Shawnee, was welcomed into the council. He had fought alongside the Wyandots during the recent Northwest Indian War. He explained to the council that despite the treaty that was signed at the conclusion of the American Revolution in 1783 in which the British ceded control of the Northwest Territory, they failed to evacuate their forts in the area.

The Northwest Territory included land between the Ohio River, the Mississippi River, and the Great Lakes. This land was home to numerous American Indian tribes. These tribes had formed a union known as the Northwest Indian Confederation to defend themselves against the encroaching settlers determined to have their land. The Confederation consisted of Shawnee, Delaware, Ottawa, Iroquois, Ojibwa, Miami, and Potawatomi. They had clashed with the Americans for the past twenty years. After two unsuccessful campaigns to eliminate the threat of the Confederation, President George Washington changed his approach in dealing with the unrest. Military reforms included expanding the army under the direction of Major General Anthony Wayne, who earned the nickname of "Mad Anthony" during his exploits in the Revolutionary War. Wayne spent two years training his men.

After listening to Simon Girty, Spirit Warrior talked to his council and pleaded with his warriors to not join the Confederation. He knew it was a losing battle. He would need every man to help defend his village if attacked. Wildcat and a few other warriors were not happy that their chief would not join the Confederation. They left the longhouse in anger, gathered their weapons and supplies, and took off through the woods to join Blue Jacket. The warriors of the Confederation regularly raided camps and settlements in the Northwest Territory, and the chiefs were confident that they could defeat any U.S. army that ventured into the region, especially after their recent victories against the Americans. They hoped the British would provide support against the Americans, as they had promised.

Girty reminded the council of the recent defeat at Fort Recovery. A large group of Northwest Indians had attacked Fort Recovery in June of 1794 but were no match for the Americans. Wayne's troops wintered at Fort Greeneville, halting movement until the spring. The leaders of the Confederation were Miami chief Little Turtle, Shawnee chief Blue Jacket and Lenape chief Buckongahelas. The failed assault on Fort Recovery bothered Little Turtle, and he asked the other chiefs to consider negotiations with the Americans. They refused. Little Turtle refused to lead the allied Indian force if negotiations were not an option and ceded his command to Blue Jacket.

At the end of the Council, Girty asked Spirit Warrior and any other warriors who were tired of fighting to join him in Canada. He had been given land by the British Crown for his service in the Northwest Indian War. He would be glad to share his land with his Shawnee brothers.

Spirit Warrior hesitated before he answered. "Thank you, my brother, we will stay here for now."

It was a decision he would regret. They had no way of knowing what was happening close to their village.

Blue Jacket found a clearing covered in fallen trees from a recent tornado and decided to camp nearby in hopes the trees would hinder the enemy. Wayne and his men were camped nearby and were expected to be on their way to engage in battle. Blue Jacket planned to ambush the Americans. A few hundred of his warriors had left to find food on the morning of the battle, not expecting any troop movement so early. U.S. scouts detected the Indians in the clearing on August 19. The next day Wayne decided to proceed with his troops toward the Northwest Indian Confederation encampment. Wayne lost many of his men to desertion but had the Kentucky volunteer cavalry as reinforcements.

The Indians attacked the Americans at nine o'clock in the morning, and as Blue Jacket had hoped, the fallen trees made it difficult for the calvary and mounted dragoons to proceed. Wayne ordered his men to make a bayonet charge into the Indian lines. The warriors retreated from their position and were chased down by the mounted forces. Surviving Indians reached Fort Miami and begged the British to let them in, but the commander refused. The promised support did not happen. The warriors of the Northwest Indian Confederation scattered. Once Wayne realized the British would not help their allies, he and his men torched the surrounding villages and crops, including Spirit Warrior's village.

The Battle of Fallen Timbers was the last major conflict between the Native Americans and the United States for control of the Northwest Territory. When the Treaty of Greenville was signed the following year, much of the area that was to become Ohio was ceded to the Americans, forcing the Native Americans to give up their land once again.

Chapter 36

BROKEN PROMISES

August 1794

It did not matter to Mad Anthony Wayne or his men that Spirit Warrior had tried to make peace between his people and the Americans. Spirit Warrior had begged the Shawnee to negotiate with the Americans and tried to stop the Northwest Confederation from striking out against the settlements. After the Battle of Fallen Timbers, Wayne and his men raided villages, burning them and destroying everything in sight. There were few warriors in camp when the attack on Spirit Warrior's village began, as most had sided with Blue Jacket. The Americans entered the village, burning wigwams, not caring if there were women or children inside. Spirit Warrior and the few remaining warriors did their best to defend their village, but they were outnumbered. Lalawethika was with his father when the assault began. Both men had one goal in mind: get to the longhouse where Sister Wolf was helping Lalawethika's wife deliver their son.

Sister Wolf had her hands full as she tended to her son's wife during the delivery. The young woman had gone into labor the previous night but did not deliver her son until just before the attack on their village. The older woman cut and tied off the cord and wrapped the little one in a cloth bundle that she tied to her chest. She knew it was just a matter of time before the longhouse they were in would be in danger. She turned her attention to the young mother, who was still bleeding. At that moment she felt a cold chill go down her spine, and she lost her vision for a few seconds. When it returned, what she saw was similar to the vision she'd had when Charles died. Both Spirit Warrior and Lalwethika were making their way toward the longhouse but were cut down by the Americans. Both fought valiantly, knowing what was at stake. Tomahawk in one hand, knife in the other, Sister Wolf's husband and son did all they could to get to her, both killing at least two men in their struggle. She watched in her mind's eye as shots rang out, and at the same time the only family she had left died, just as her husband, father, and son had twenty years before. A stray bullet pierced the skull of her son's wife as Sister Wolf's son and husband were shot by Wayne's men only a few feet from the door. Just after Sister Wolf's grandson made his entrance into this world, her beloved husband, son, and her son's wife made their exit. Sister Wolf regained her eyesight only to see the lifeless eyes of the mother of her grandson.

For a moment it was more than she could bear, but she knew she could not give in to her pain. There was nothing she could do about those who had fallen. Her first priority was the baby. She must hurry! She knew she needed to get out of the longhouse, but it was going to be difficult. Mary Sister Wolf could not believe what was going on. Surely, she was being punished for something. She did not have to go outside to know that all of her family was dead except for the tiny one she clung to.

Sister Wolf had one important task: to keep this newborn baby tied to her chest alive and get him out of the village. She gently touched the head of his mother, said a quick prayer, and grabbed her bundle. It took all of her strength and effort to lift the door flap, look outside to see the carnage around her, and run toward the woods to find a safe place for her grandson.

By now most of the village had been torched. For some reason Wayne's men had moved away from the longhouse, burning and looting as they went. She knew her husband and son were lying nearby but could not risk looking for their bodies now; she had to get out of her village. It was if she were invisible to the white men as she quickly moved away from the longhouse and toward the cover of the woods. If only she could reach the nearby cave, the one she had discovered the year she and Spirit Warrior set up their first wigwam. She had spent hours with her son there, showing him how to live in a cave, how to disguise the opening, and how to build a small fire. Thankfully, she still had some supplies stashed in the cave. It would at least give her and her precious grandson a chance to survive.

When Sister Wolf reached the small opening of the cave, she turned to make sure she had not been followed. The entire village was blazing in a red-hot fire. She was numb with pain. How could this be happening again? Her heart was beating so quickly that she thought it would explode in her chest. Part of her wished it would, but the part of her that had promised to love her husband, her son, and now her grandson would not let her give up. She must survive this and be there for the little one she held.

The most important thing Sister Wolf needed was milk for the baby. It had been too many years since she had nursed her son, as his wife would have her own son. She would wait until the morning to see if there were any white men left in her village. She needed to find the bodies of her husband and son—it was futile to believe they might still be alive—and also look for a goat that might have escaped the needless killing and destruction of the day.

It was all the woman could do not to give in to her need to scream to release the madness in her mind, but she could not risk being found. Sister Wolf rocked and held the baby, whispering promises to him that she would take care of him. At that moment she thought of the promises she had made and others had made to her in years past. She allowed her mind to drift back to Mohan's Camp and thought of her vows to Charles and his to her during their hand fasting. She thought of the day her world was destroyed. Charles had promised her that he and her father would not be gone long when they left that morning to hunt. He promised! The British had promised the Indians they would help them fend off the Americans pouring into their hunting grounds but turned their backs on them when they needed their help the most. Mary remembered the promise she made during the funeral for her father, her husband Charles, and her son Ryan. She had promised to kill Digging Turtle and she did. She looked into the eyes of the precious baby in her arms and promised him again that she would take care of him. She was all he had, and he was all she had. Her world was destroyed again, and she did not know how she would keep her promise; she just knew that she would. She prayed to the Creator to help her keep this baby alive and to accept the spirits of her husband and son.

Chapter 37

ANSWERED PRAYERS

August 1794

Mary Sister Wolf wrapped her grandson in the cloth, tied the bundle to her chest, and quickly left the cave above her village. She needed to look for her husband and son. Although she knew in her heart they were dead, she still must face what she knew awaited her. Hopefully, Wayne and his men were gone, and she could find some milk for the baby. The village was still smoldering, smoke rising from the wigwams and longhouses.

At first Mary could not believe that she heard the cries of a young woman. She had assumed that anyone left in the village was dead. As she cautiously approached what was left of a wigwam, she heard the young woman again. She was lying on the ground, blood everywhere. As the older woman bent to speak to her, she recognized Morning Dove, a cousin of her husband, Spirit Warrior. She had recently given birth to a baby girl, and Mary quickly looked in the wigwam to see if the baby was there. She was, but she was dead. Her heart was breaking; she did not know how much more she could take.

Mary quickly checked Morning Dove for injuries, did what she could to stop the bleeding, and helped her to the longhouse not far away. Unbelievably, it was still standing. She wondered why the young mother did not ask about her baby, but it was soon apparent that she had seen her daughter and knew she was dead. Mary explained that she needed to check for her husband and son, but Morning Dove started crying. She explained that they tried to defend her when Wayne's men began torching her wigwam. That is when they were shot. They were lying behind her wigwam with her husband, who was also dead. The white men clubbed her and her baby, then set the wigwam on fire.

The baby tied to Mary's chest began to cry. Morning Dove looked in amazement as Mary unwrapped him and placed him in the young woman's arms. Without being asked, the young mother offered her breast to the hungry baby. It saved his life. Mary thanked her and promised to be back shortly. She must look after her family.

Sister Wolf knew what she would find, but she was a warrior and a chief's wife. She had to be brave and face the gruesome sight she knew was waiting for her behind Morning Dove's wigwam. As she reached the back of the wigwam, she fell to her knees, screaming in pain. There on the ground was Spirit Warrior, shot through the heart. Beside him lay their son, also shot through the heart. Morning Dove's husband was close by, shot in the head. If not for the baby in Morning Dove's arms, Mary would have ended her life right there, but she knew she was needed and had to find the strength to do what she must do to survive. At least the three men had not suffered, as they had died instantly, but why? None of these people had joined in the battle against Mad Anthony Wayne. She felt the urge to avenge these deaths just as she had with Digging Turtle.

Just then Mary heard voices, voices speaking in Shawnee. A few of the warriors who had joined Blue Jacket had returned to the village. She forced herself not to scream at them, to ask them how they could leave their own people defenseless. One of the warriors, Wildcat, approached her cautiously. He quickly saw his chief and the chief's son on the ground in front of Sister Wolf. He could not look her in the eyes; he was ashamed. Tears ran down his cheeks as he vowed to avenge their deaths. She calmed down and explained that right now she needed help with the bodies that were strewn all over their village. Wildcat gathered the warriors in the center of the village and explained that they needed to check for any survivors and bury their dead.

Sister Wolf and Morning Dove remained in the village as the warriors went about their difficult tasks. There were only a handful of survivors. Sister Wolf helped when she could with those who were injured and with the bodies of the dead. She performed a mass Crossing Over Ceremony for the dead, including her husband and son. Then she had a decision to make: stay here with the Shawnee or go back to Mohan's Camp. Both sides had caused her so much pain. Both sides had taken away her family. She loved and hated both the white man and the Indians. Where did she fit in now?

Sister Wolf knew what she must do—leave the Shawnee, as they would be pushed out of this area—and return to Mohan's Camp. She would take Morning Dove with her if she wanted to go, and together they would try to make a life for themselves in her previous home.

The two women hated to leave the Shawnee village. It had been their home, but their families were dead, and they needed to make the best of what life had thrown their way. Sister Wolf knew that the Shawnee way of life was never going to be the same again. With

Morning Dove's help, she knew she could raise her grandson, whom she named Michael Little Hawk after her father and uncle.

It had been over twenty years since the red-haired lass had left Mohan's Camp, and she had no idea if it would even be there, but if the Mohan brothers were still there, she was sure they would be welcomed. The two women gathered their belongings, and at least now they had two horses to ride to make the trip easier. Before they left the village, Mary visited the graves of her husband and son and prayed for a safe journey east. She prayed for the strength to face each day without them and to be able to raise her grandson. She offered tobacco, placing it on the ground, looked one last time at their graves, then got on her horse and the two women started their journey east.

Mary Sister Wolf was happy to have Morning Dove's company and her assistance in feeding her grandson. The trip eastward was much easier with the horses. As they got closer to their destination, Mary recognized the hill where the ancient ones had opened up access to the underground spring. They stopped there to fill their water bags and for Morning Dove to feed the baby. Mary knew they were close now. She hoped and prayed that the Mohans would welcome them as they had before.

Mary Sister Wolf's fears were unfounded. The Mohan brothers had received word that she was on her way to their camp, and they made sure her old cabin was ready for her. The two women settled into a routine, taking care of the baby, planting a garden, cooking, cleaning, whatever needed to be done. The camp had grown since Mary had been there last. There were more people, some who did not hold a grudge against Native Americans but also some who did.

Mary dealt with them as she had always dealt with difficult people: she faced them head on, never intimidated by anyone, man, or woman. As much as she embraced her connection to the Shawnee, she thought it better to call her grandson by his Christian name, Michael, and not his Shawnee name, Little Hawk.

It was not long before Morning Dove caught the eye of one of the men who worked for the Mohans, Richard Falls' son, David. They were married and she moved into his cabin near Buffalo Creek. Michael was growing like a weed and was a delight to his grandmother and helped her deal with her losses. He thrived in the cabin his grandmother had shared with her first husband, Charles. For Mary, it brought back so many memories, and although it was painful, it also gave her a feeling of being home, of being grounded.

The years passed quickly. Michael grew into a strong, dependable young man, as his father and grandfather were before him. The area also grew and became known as the Forks of the Buffalo. People were building cabins, and eventually, a town called Koon Town grew up west of the Mohans' camp. Michael soon fell in love with a local girl, Sarah West, and they were married. Thankfully, they stayed close to his grandmother, who was getting on in years but was still a strong, capable woman. In the spring of 1828, Michael and Sarah were blessed with a son, Matthew.

Unfortunately, young Sarah died during the birth of her son. Michael never got over his loss. He never remarried, and his grandmother took over the job of raising her great-grandson. Michael added on to his grandmother's cabin to make room for them all to live together but remained distant to both his son and grandmother.

Michael announced one morning that he was leaving the next day to join the fighting in the Mexican American War. No amount of pleading from his grandmother could sway him; he was determined to go. She tried to reason with him, explain that his son needed him, but to no avail. Michael's reasoning was that his son was not a child, he was a man of eighteen and did not need his father. That was in May of 1846. Michael lost his life in the Battle of Buena Vista in February of 1847. His grandmother never got over it. Thankfully, her great-grandson, Matthew, was dedicated to her and stayed with her in their cabin on Mohan's Run.

Chapter 38

ODDS AND ENDS

As the months and years passed since Michael died and the raising of his son, Matthew, fell upon his great-grandmother, the two became remarkably close. Mary delighted in teaching the young man skills that had been forgotten by many, skills she had learned from her elders. Matthew could track better than anyone in the area, knew about the plants that had been used as medicine, and was as good at shooting as his beloved "GG." At the end of the day, while cleaning up after their evening meal, Mary would tell young Matthew about the people she had met after arriving from Ireland. Some were local white men, others were Shawnee she knew from her time living with them.

One of Mary's favorite stories was about Nonhelema, or Katherine as she was sometimes known. She was a Shawnee warrior and chief who just happened to be a woman. She was the daughter of Okowellos and her mother, Katee, was Métis. She had been married to a Chalakatha Shawnee chief. Later, she had a son with a white captive named Richard Butler, also known as Captain Butler or Tamanatha. She also had a son named Thomas McKee through her relationship with an Indian agent named Colonel Alexander McKee. Her last relationship was with the Shawnee chief Moluntha. The two women met when Cornstalk and Nonhelema met with Spirit Warrior to find a peaceful solution to the problems between the Shawnee, the British, and the Americans.

Nonhelema and Sister Wolf were very much alike, except in height. Both could be fierce warriors and yet knew in their hearts that peace was the only way their people would survive. Sister Wolf looked up to her sister warrior, and they enjoyed a deep friendship for years. Telling of Nonhelema's last years on earth always brought tears to her eyes.

After the Battle of Bushy Run, Nonhelema was convinced that Shawnee survival depended on peace. She and her brother, Cornstalk, supported neutrality. During the Revolutionary War, she and Cornstalk tried to help make peace, while other Shawnees aided the British. She served as a guide and translator. After Cornstalk was murdered in 1777, she left her tribe to support the Americans. She warned Fort Randolph of a Shawnee attack in 1778. Her herd of cattle and horses were destroyed during that siege. She negotiated with the attackers for the fort and disguised messengers who were sent to warn Fort Donnally of a possible Shawnee attack. She served as a guide and translator in 1780 for Lieutenant Colonel Augustin Mottin de la Balme, the U.S. inspector general of cavalry, when he traveled to Illinois to trade with the Indians.

Nonhelema petitioned Congress in 1785 for a 1,000-acre grant of land in Ohio as compensation for her service during the Revolutionary War and the loss of her livestock. Congress, instead, voted her a pension of daily rations for life and an annual allotment of a set of clothes and a blanket. In 1786, when General Benjamin Logan led Kentucky militia against the Ohio Shawnee, Nonhelema and her husband and family surrendered to the troops. After they were in custody, a soldier killed Moluntha, and Nonhelema was detained in Pittsburgh. While at Fort Pitt, she helped the commander compile a Shawnee dictionary. She died sometime after her release in December of 1786.

Mary also told Matthew of some of the local men she had known who had experienced tragedies at the hands of Indians. Just as her father, Michael, had realized, she too knew there was good and bad in both cultures. Hermit Eeds was the first man she met who had spent his life killing Indians. She told Matthew of the cave nearby that Eeds had shown her, the one where Matthew had loved tracing the drawings on the walls with his little fingers.

Another local man, Lewis Wetzel, had moved near the Ohio River, close to Fort Henry, with his parents and siblings in 1770. The area was remote, and the settlers were in constant conflict with Native American tribes. In 1777, Lewis, thirteen, and his younger brother Jacob, eleven, were captured by Wyandot Indians. Lewis and Jacob were working in the fields with their father and older brother. They were sent back to the cabin and were attacked as they left the cabin to return to the field. Lewis was hit in the chest by a gunshot, tearing away a piece of his sternum.

The brothers were taken across the Ohio River. On their third night of captivity, the boys slipped out of their bonds and made their escape. Their shoes had been taken from them to help prevent their escape. Young Lewis returned to the Indian camp, stole two pairs of moccasins, his father's rifle, powder horn, and shot pouch. The brothers then escaped back across the river.

Lewis practiced shooting and could hit anything with a single shot. He was a natural athlete, quick, agile, and could run fast and for long distances. Legend has it that Lewis taught himself how to load, prime, and shoot his rifle while running at full speed through the woods.

Due to the treatment he was given by the Indians as a boy, and later the death of his father and brother at the hands of Indians, Wetzel developed a deep hatred of all Indians. Within a year of his capture, he had begun to enact violent attacks against the Ohio Indians, taking scalps.

Mary was quiet as she thought of what young Wetzel had gone through, losing family members, much like she had. She understood his need for revenge. It was one of the memories she struggled with through the years.

Frontier warfare was brutal. Native tribes allied themselves with the British during the American Revolution to stem the tide of the whites encroaching into their lands in the Ohio River Valley. There were raids and counterraids. Peaceful Indians were slaughtered and white captives were tortured in retaliation. The frontier society where Wetzel grew up considered the killing of Indians to be a public service. Pioneer families considered him a hero; he defended them against the Indian threat. Others regarded him as a sociopathic killer. He was described as six feet tall with jet-black eyes and long dark hair that he wore in braids. He grew his hair long to taunt those who sought his scalp. He had no permanent home, no labor other than hunting or guiding and protecting land speculators and surveyors. There was no steady woman in his life. Lewis Wetzel was an Indian killer, not an Indian fighter. He did not hesitate to murder Indians in cold blood. The Indians called him "Death Wind."

After killing and scalping a peaceful Seneca chief in the late 1780s, Wetzel was caught and brought back to Fort Harmer, where he managed to escape. He was arrested again and was jailed at Fort Washington. A mob of 200 frontiersmen assembled, demanding his release. Among them was Simon Kenton. A judge released Wetzel, who then took off for Spanish Louisiana, where it was reported that he engaged in counterfeiting and spent time in a Spanish prison. He died in 1808 in Mississippi.

Mary remembered Hermit Eeds telling her about his friend John Ice. John preferred to stay away from most people and stayed mostly to himself. Eads was his friend, perhaps because they were so much alike. Both men hated Indians and spent their life taking revenge for their lost loved ones.

John Ice had lived in hell on earth, and he was determined to make those responsible pay for their actions. He was not an easy man to get along with, perhaps because so much had been taken from him. John was the son of Frederick Ice and Mary Galloway Ice. While living in the South Branch Valley of Virginia, the Indians took his mother, two sisters, and his brother hostage. John and his father, Frederick, searched for their missing family for years. His mother was never found. By the time his sisters were found, they preferred to continue living with their captors. His brother, "Indian" Billy, lived with the Shawnee for a time but eventually returned to his white family. John later said that the Indians killed his mother and his sweetheart.

Frederick Ice later remarried and settled on the Cheat River at what is now known as Ice's Ferry. John Ice eventually moved to the Forks of the Buffalo, present-day Mannington, West Virginia. If not the first resident of this area, he was one of the first.

Ice was known for his tracking abilities and alerted the residents when Indians were in the area, so they could find safety in one of the local forts.

At one point, Ice owned much of the land in the area at the Forks of the Buffalo. Eventually, he sold off pieces of his land and he became caretaker to land owned by others who did not live in the area. Those absentee owners were Robert Rutherford and future president James Madison.

A group of renegades called the "Whiskey Boys" started giving Ice trouble once he became caretaker for the absent landowners. He was trying to clear them out of the area when he and Jim Snodgrass died in 1797. Most people blamed the Indians, but there were people who believed they were killed by the ruffians, the undesirables John Ice tried to keep from the lands he protected. The Mohans believed John Ice and Jim Snodgrass were murdered at Fishing Creek by the Whiskey Boys, who made it look like Indians had killed them.

Chapter 39

THE DREAM

January 14, 1848

Matthew tried to sleep but it was difficult. His great-grandmother, whom he called GG, was lying in her bed, obviously extremely ill and not expected to live. There was nothing left that could be done for her. He had done what she had asked, played her hand drum, sang her songs, comforted her when she woke from her deep sleep. He finally drifted off to sleep in the middle of the night. It was then that Matthew had the most unbelievable experience of his young life—he thought he was awake, but he could not move or speak. He was sitting in a chair beside Mary's bed and was startled when he saw his GG turn to look at him. When she did, she smiled. She was no longer ninety-five years old; she was twenty! Her hair was bright auburn. She got out of bed, opened the door, and walked out to the oak tree in the yard. Waiting for her was a magnificent warrior! It had to be Spirit Warrior, his great-grandfather. Who else could it be? He saw them talking briefly and saw Spirit Warrior give her his necklace. GG had a feather in her hand after stroking his hair. All this time a beautiful silver wolf stood beside his GG. They embraced, then the warrior and the wolf turned to walk into the woods. It was then that the wolf howled. Mary walked back into the cabin but left the door open. She climbed back into bed as if nothing had happened.

Matthew thought he went back to sleep but was awakened when he saw a young man walk into the room. Again, Matthew could not speak or move. It was if the man did not see him. Mary smiled at the man, then sat up in the bed. When she did, the young man hugged her, then kissed her. They had a conversation that Matthew could not hear, then the man pulled a purple flower from his bag and gave it to his GG. It was almost more than he could bear but Matthew was helpless to do anything. What was happening? He drifted off to sleep.

Chapter 40

THE CROSSING OVER

January 15, 1848

Matthew awoke, feeling the frigid air on his face. For a moment he forgot where he was and what was happening. Then he remembered he was in the cabin of his great-grandmother Mary Sister Wolf Ryan McLain, who was on her death bed. He had spent part of the night singing the songs she loved, drumming the song he knew she would need to cross over to the other side, and holding her hand until he fell asleep. The freezing air brought him back to the present, and he realized the cabin door was standing wide open. Matthew quickly shut the door as he saw snowflakes flying about the cabin. One landed softly on his great-grandmother's lips, but it did not melt. It was then that he knew she was gone

Matthew reached to touch her hand, only to feel the cold-stone hardness of a lifeless body. As much as he knew she was ready to go, he had not been ready to let her go. He watched as the snowflake finally melted, not because of the touch of a warm body but because the cabin was still warmer inside than it was outside. It was then he saw it: a necklace in her left hand. That was strange. It had not been there last night, he was sure of it. The necklace jarred his memory. He remembered having a dream last night in which he saw his grandmother standing beside the oak tree near the cabin, talking to his great-grandfather. He did not hear the words they spoke, only saw them embrace, and then his great-grandfather removed the necklace around his neck and gave it to his wife, Matthew's great-grandmother. She in turn stroked his hair, and when she did, the eagle feather tied in her husband's dark hair fell into her hand.

Matthew reached across her body, gently pried her fingers from the beaded necklace, and saw what his grandmother had described to him often in the past: the necklace she had made for her Shawnee husband for their wedding day. That was impossible; she had told him it had been buried with the body. His mind reeled with what he saw. For a moment he was back in time, a young boy sitting at his great-grandmother's knee, taking in all that she said. She was a wise woman, and he learned much from her in those early years. Before he could begin to process the idea that his great-grandmother had been holding an object that had been buried with his great-grand-father, he thought of the dream, and it was then that he saw the feather in her right hand.

It was more than the young man could comprehend: there, in her right hand, was an eagle feather. He did not know what to think. It was not possible! Was he losing his mind? Was someone playing a cruel trick on him? He could not have seen his great-grandpar-ents last night by the oak tree—they were both dead—but he could not deny the fact that she held the same objects in her hands that he had seen in his dream. In his dream Mary had also had other visitors. Her first husband, Charles, had walked through the open door to the cabin after the warrior left. He visited with Mary, held her close, then gave her a purple flower, as he had done years ago.

Matthew looked on her pillow. The purple flower was by her head. Matthew said, half aloud, "The only thing missing is her wolf." He had seen the wolf also in his dream, standing by the tree, watching his great-grandparents embrace. He had heard the wolf howl before it took off into the darkness with his great-grandfather.

Matthew rose to put the necklace, feather, and flower on the dresser, and as he did, he heard a wolf howl. He knew it! He *had* heard it last night; it wasn't a dream. Without thinking, he grabbed for his grandmother's old muzzle loader as he stepped out onto the porch to see for himself. If it was a wolf, his grandmother would not have allowed him to shoot it, but grabbing the gun was instinct on his part. He looked down the hill toward the spot where the Mohans' camp had been. He thought he saw movement in the brush. He turned back toward the cabin, thinking of the woman lying on the bed, but he could do nothing for her now. He closed the door to the cabin and said to his great-grandmother the same thing he had said a thousand times before when he left her. "I love you, GG, I'll be back." He had to see about the wolf.

As Matthew made his way down the path, memories flooded his head: the stories of the wolf, his great-grandfather Spirit Warrior, his mother's adopted family, Red Hawk, White Feather, and Walking Owl. He knew all the stories of the days when this was really a wilderness, and he loved them all.

Matthew reached the bottom of the hill in a couple of minutes. He was still young and muscular like his father and grandfather had been. He rounded the path near the site of the old camp and stopped in his tracks as he saw the beautiful silver wolf standing there before him. He knew he shouldn't look it in the eyes but couldn't help it. The wolf stared back at him. Their eyes locked, and Matthew spoke to it, "Hello, Brother Wolf, I am glad to finally meet you." He wasn't sure why he said that, it just seemed like the right thing to do. The wolf looked up the hill toward the cabin and howled. It startled Matthew, but he didn't move. "Would you like to say goodbye to her?" he asked. As if he knew what the young man had said, the wolf started up the path to the cabin, Matthew following behind him.

When they reached the front porch, the wolf stopped and let Matthew go past him to open the door. "I must be out of my mind," Matthew said aloud. The two walked into the cabin and the wolf went straight to the bed. If anyone saw him now, Matthew thought, they would think he had lost his mind, but it was as if he knew this was what his grandmother wanted. The wolf went to the old woman's bedside, sniffed her, then climbed up on the bed, circled twice, and then curled up beside her, his head on her chest. Matthew didn't know what to do now. If this was *her* wolf, which was impossible, he knew it would leave as soon as it came to do whatever it was supposed to do. If it was a wild wolf, which no doubt it was, it could start to eat his grandmother and hurt him. He must be dreaming.

Matthew watched, looking for signs that the big wolf was going to do something other than lie by his great-grandmother as if mourning her loss. After a couple of minutes, the wolf lifted its head, licked the old woman's face a couple of times, then turned and looked at the young man sitting in the chair. Tears welled up in the young man's eyes as he stood up. The wolf jumped down from the bed, came to Matthew, and jumped, putting his front paws on

Matthew's shoulders. It all happened so fast, too fast for Matthew to react if he was in danger. But he didn't feel the wolf was a threat to him, as unbelievable as that seemed. The wolf began to lick the tears from Matthew's face, and as he did, Matthew hugged the wolf and began to cry even harder. For a moment it seemed as if they communicated with each other, just as the wolf had done with his GG. As quickly as he had arrived, the wolf turned and walked onto the porch, and as he did, he turned and looked at both Matthew and the old woman and howled. It was a sound Matthew would never forget.

The big male wolf turned, jumped from the porch, and ran into the woods above the cabin. For a moment Matthew stood in disbelief of what he had just seen. How could he explain this to anyone? No one would believe him, even the people who had known Mary Sister Wolf Ryan McLain and knew of the unexplainable events that happened when she was around would not believe this. Matthew still didn't.

The sun was beginning to come up in the east, his grandmother's favorite time of the day. It was when she stopped to take a moment to thank the Creator for her blessings, her family, and her friends. She would come out on the porch, no matter how cold it was, face the east, and recite her morning prayer. "Thank You, Creator, for another day. Thank You for all my blessings, especially my family and friends. Guide us and watch over us today and every day. Thank You, A'ho."

Matthew began to recite the old woman's prayer. As he finished he looked at the oak tree just off the porch. As he walked toward it, he saw three sets of footprints: one large, one smaller, and what looked like wolf prints between them. There were no tracks leading to or from the tree, just the three sets of prints in the snow. As the young man stood there staring at the three sets of prints, the sun rose above the hill to the east of the cabin, sending the most beautiful light, filtered through the tree, to shine on them, creating a bright glint reflected on the snow. Matthew stood there, tears running down his face as he said, "I love you, GG!"

A soft wind blew across his face as he heard his great-grandmother's voice say, "I love you too, Matthew. I will always be with you," and then the wolf howled from the woods.

It was at that moment that he knew his great-grandmother was with her loved ones, her parents, Michael, and Mary Ryan, her first husband, Charles, their son, Ryan, Matthew's parents and grandparents, and his great-grandfather Spirit Warrior. They all walked towards the west, the wolf guiding their way. Mary Sister Wolf had Crossed Over.